Red Dragon's Keep

Natli VanDerWerken

Zenith Star Publishing

Aurora, Colorado

Published by Zenith Star Publishing
1505 S Norfolk St
Aurora, CO 80017
303 755-5404 (Office)
natli@natlivanderwerken.com

Cover Design © 2017 Natli VanDerWerken.com

Book Layout © 2017 BookDesignTemplates.com

Books may be purchased for sales promotion by contacting the publisher.

Red Dragon's Keep/ Natli VanDerWerken -- 1st ed.
ISBN 978-0-9991750-0-2   (paperback)
ISBN 978-0-9991750-1-9   (ePub)
ISBN 978-0-9991750-2-6   (audiobook)

Library of Congress Control Number: 2017910528

Dedication

To my sister Peg
and my daughters, Anne, Debbie and Jenni.
Without you, this book would never have been written.

To my husband Dan, who always, always, had my back.

Finalist in the 2016 AuthorU
'Draft to Dream' Contest

I'm a retired and substitute teacher in my local school district. When I read the beginning chapters of Red Dragon's Keep to my second and fourth grade students, you could have heard a pin drop. As I paused to turn a page on my phone, one of the students said "Can't you read faster?" This is a great book for YA readers.

Richard Goben, Retired Teacher

Contents

Map of Ard An Tir

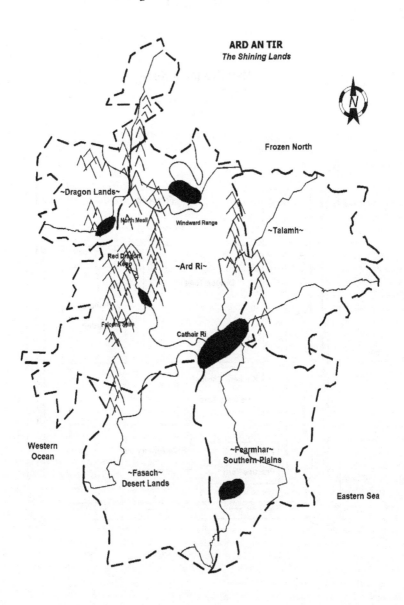

ARD AN TIR
The Shining Lands

Frozen North

~Dragon Lands~

North Meall

Windward Range

~Talamh~

Red Dragon Keep

~Ard Ri~

Falcons Spire

Cathair Ri

Western Ocean

~Fearmhar~
Southern Plains

~Fasach~
Desert Lands

Eastern Sea

Map of Red Dragon's Keep

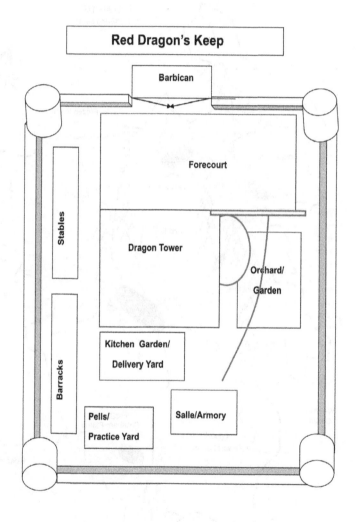

Map of First Demon Battle

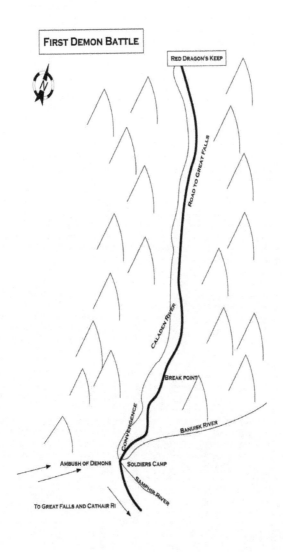

Prologue

Far away and long ago...

In her human form, Fire bowed low to the Rí, the King of the Dragons. The King's black scales grated against the tiles of the forecourt as he shifted his bulk.

"To what do I owe this honor, my Lord?" she asked, giving a short formal bow.

The walls of Dragon Tower in the center of Red Dragon's Keep stood grim and dark sentinel as evening twilight deepened. The last light of day reflected from the billowing storm clouds retreating to the east, highlighting the red Dragon laid in stone up the Tower's east wall.

"The time has come, my daughter," his voice echoed in her mind. *"We and the humans have won against the Ciardha. The humans will become strong and look askance at our dominance. We must withdraw to the strongholds to avoid the conflict that I see in the future. I cannot compel you. You must choose."*

Cold wind swirled over the walls and into the forecourt. The short hairs on the back of Fire's neck lifted. A shiver raced down her spine. Hair escaping the braid down her back fluttered around her face.

"Know this. If your choice is to stay, you will lose all knowledge of what you are. Magic shall still be yours, but you will not know why you have it, nor any of your history. You will be locked from Dragon form until the need is so great that you must take it. The choice is yours."

Fire gazed at the huge black Dragon who was her King, her father. She knew the law. Each of the Dragons was free to choose whether to stay or go. Most had chosen to go.

Stubbornly she dropped her eyes and shook her head. *"My Ri, I choose to stay. The Arachs shall need my help in the times ahead. I am bound to them as you were bound to the human King."*

The great black Dragon closed his eyes and bowed his head. *"As you will it."* Pain choked his voice. *"Long life, daughter."*

He spread his immense wings and slammed them down…once…twice, shoving dust and dead leaves heaped around the forecourt into a whirlwind. Thunder rumbled. He rose above the Keep wall with its red Dragon laid out in stone and turned to the west.

In time to the rhythm of his flight, he wove his magic. His voice echoed in her mind again. *"As I fly, all knowledge of your past slips free. Farewell, my child."* Then he was gone.

Fire, pale and sick at heart, watched him dwindle away.

She felt oddly out of focus.

Why am I in the forecourt?

She frowned and glanced around, searching her memory. She shook her head, trying to clear it.

She turned and walked back into the Tower.

Chapter 1

"Thomas! Stop that!"

Startled, Thomas lost his grip and dropped the sword he was swinging back and forth onto the stones of the forecourt. He spun toward Duke Tom Arach, his father, and hung his head.

The Duke turned from the sergeant who held his horse by the reins. Taller than most men, the Duke was broad-shouldered and fit, his red-gold hair was plastered to his head by sweat. A greying red-gold mustache and goatee framed a strong mouth and chin. Skin weathered brown by much time spent in the sun streamed more sweat. He carried his helmet in the crook of his heavily muscled left arm. He'd been out practicing battle maneuvers and his horse had thrown a shoe.

"Look at me. What are you thinking? You know you're not supposed to be using swords," barked his father. "Now pick that up and take it back to the armory," he continued, his blue eyes sharp under frowning brows. He shook his head at Thomas and waved his hand toward the Dragon Tower and the armory behind it. He turned back to the sergeant.

Thomas bent down and retrieved the sword, now nicked by the paving stones of the forecourt, and slid it into the scabbard that he carried in his left hand. His sun-streaked dark blond hair fell over his blue eyes, and he brushed it back impatiently. He looked at his father.

"I'm sorry. I was coming to ask if you could teach me. Captain Mathin helped me pick this one. I was going to ask if it was okay."

The Duke turned toward him again. "Thomas, I can't do it right now. I don't have time. The King has ordered your mother, me and your aunt and uncle to the capital, Cathair Ri. War is coming. No, take it back to the armory." He shook his head.

Thomas froze in disappointment. *Just like always. I never get to do things with Father. I never get to do things that I want to, period.*

"Yes sir." Thomas turned on his heel and marched back through the forecourt, shoulders straight, back rigid. He refused to let his father see how hurt he felt.

He marched through the arch that opened to the left of the Tower wall. As soon as he was out of sight, his shoulders slumped. He shook his head in frustration. Everything he did turned out to be the wrong thing. His parents had always treated him like he might die if he did anything they thought was dangerous. He pulled the sword from its sheath again with a rebellious tug.

He followed the curving path around the side of the shorter Lady's Tower to the armory. Dense shade under the fruit trees lining the path gave some small relief from the oppressive heat. It radiated from the paving stones, almost burning his feet through his sturdy leather boots. Soon summer would turn to fall and he knew that the cold would curl his toes.

Pulling the left side of the heavy oak doors open, Thomas stepped into the welcome cool of the salle, the large room in front of the armory where squires were taught how to fight, both armed and unarmed.

He paused uncertainly in the doorway. Captain Mathin stood facing a tall slender woman. Lady Aeden cocked her head to the side, as if questioning what the captain was telling her.

Thomas tried to walk silently as he had seen the better soldiers in his father's guard move. His heel caught on one of the bricks in the uneven floor surrounding the training surface and he stumbled forward, almost falling. The sword hit the floor again.

Humiliated at his clumsiness, his face burning, Thomas closed his eyes and just stood, waiting for the verbal abuse he knew was coming. The salle was deathly silent. Opening his eyes, he looked toward the captain and Aeden. Both of them were simply staring over their shoulders at him. Aeden and Mathin glanced at each other, then turned as one to face the eldest son and heir to Red Dragon's Keep.

"What is it, Thomas?" asked Captain Mathin in a surprisingly kind voice. He was a tall, solidly built man who had served with Thomas's father during the last war. His sparse brown hair was cut short and his grey eyes held a smile.

"Father said to bring the sword back. He said that he hasn't time to teach me. He and Mother are going to the capital to meet with the King," Thomas blurted out in a rush.

Captain Mathin's eyebrows rose in surprise.

"I'd not heard. Well, put the sword up after you've sharpened it and I'll talk to the Duke about lessons for you while he's gone."

"I'm sorry, Captain Mathin. I don't know how to sharpen it. No one will let me near the swords." *Almost like they think I'll cut off my fingers or toes*, he thought bitterly.

Captain Mathin glanced at Aeden. "My Lady, would you have the time to teach Thomas how to sharpen the sword?"

A small smile lurked at one corner of Aeden's mouth. "I think I might be able to do that, Captain Mathin." She turned to Thomas and beckoned him to her.

"Right. Then I'll be off to talk to the Duke," said Captain Mathin. He turned, strode through the partially open door and pulled it shut after him. Silence again filled the salle.

Thomas had seen Lady Aeden at the Keep all of his life. She was one of the vassals sworn to his father, but she had never spoken to *him*. Aeden scouted for the guard, advised his father on defenses for the duchy and taught the squires armed and unarmed combat. She bore her title by courtesy, not by birth.

He approached her shyly and held the sword out to her.

"No, keep it and let's go to the armory," she said. Turning, she walked across the salle and he followed eagerly. *Finally, I get to learn something useful.*

Aeden watched him from the corner of her eye.

At fourteen, Thomas was tall for his age, almost as tall as his father. The boy moved well, albeit stiffly. *Still growing into himself and learning how to move,* she thought. She could teach him many things, and would, she vowed silently. She felt the power that coiled within him, and his blindness to that power. This must change, and soon. Rumors had already reached Red Dragon's Keep about Demons raiding Steadings, slaughtering those they could not turn to the Dark's service.

When they walked through the doors into the hall leading to the armory, three boys jumped to their feet. They were perhaps two or three years older than Thomas. *Squires, by the looks of them,* she thought. Thomas stumbled to a halt, looking everywhere but at the boys.

The short, thin squire bowed deeply to Aeden. The other, of medium height with an abundance of black hair falling into his blue eyes, followed suit.

The tallest squire, Garan, stocky and defiant, stood with legs spread aggressively, fingers bending the belt at his waist in half, sneering. He ignored her.

"So, sent back again, eh? When will you learn? You may be the Lord's son, but he cares nothing for you. Not even enough to teach you the sword. Give it up and get back to your nursemaid," he taunted.

Thomas flinched as if struck by a whiplash.

Aeden was shocked into immobility. How dare this young lout speak to the heir in such a manner. Her eyes widened as he continued.

"You're nothing, never have been, never will be. Your da is just a jumped up captain from the guard. Never mind he saved the King's life. So did a lot of others."

He scowled. *His* father had fought in the last war, too. The other squires stirred uneasily.

Aeden looked at Thomas. His shoulders were hunched, his face white. He cringed as if from a blow. Apparently this wasn't the first time that he'd been bullied by this squire. Dust floated in the sunbeams shining through the clerestory windows that formed the ceiling of the hall. The dust began to swirl.

Aeden spoke one quiet word.

"Stop."

Her power shivered through the armory.

"You."

She pointed at Thomas's tormentor.

"You will report, under guard, to the Duke. Now. You will tell him exactly what you said to *Lord* Thomas." She emphasized the title. "He shall have your punishment. You and you, return to the barracks."

Aeden flicked her hand at the two squires trying to shrink into invisibility. She shouted down the hallway to the guards standing at attention on either side of the armory doors.

"Privates, both of you come and escort this... person... to Duke Arach."

The soldiers started down the hallway.

Garan snorted and took a step toward her. "You have no authority here, woman. You are just a scout. Leave now and I'll forget you tried to order me anywhere."

Fear whispered in the corners of the room.

Eyes wide, the other squires backed away from the coming storm, turned and scuttled from the hallway.

Aeden's left brow rose, her blue eyes glittered. As tall as Garan, she stalked forward and slapped him hard on the right cheek and backhanded him on the left.

Garan clapped his hand to his jaw in shock. Fury narrowed his eyes. His jaw bulged as he clenched his teeth. He threw his arm up to deflect another strike and reached out with the other to grab Aeden by her tunic.

Aeden braced to take him, teeth bared, a fierce grin of anticipation widening her mouth. She moved to keep Thomas in her peripheral vision.

Thomas straightened and faced Garan. His knuckles whitened as his fingers tightened on the grip of the sword. His ears turned red with anger, his lips clamped in a thin line.

"No," he shouted, "This is the last time." He clumsily swung his sword into guard position and jumped between Garan and Aeden.

"Stop," she said again, with more force this time, as she lifted her right hand, palm out, fingers splayed. She straightened from her crouch.

Garan was frozen where he stood, his face contorting with panic. Thomas tried to lower his sword and could not.

"Your courage in my defense is admirable, Lord Thomas. Thank you," she said with a small bow to him. "Enough." She gestured as if pulling on a rope and Garan stumbled toward her.

Thomas was finally able to slowly lower the tip of his sword to the ground, his eyes wide and mouth open in astonishment.

With negligent ease, Aeden kicked Garan's feet out from under him. As he landed hard on his back on the floor she whispered, "Stay. You will remain here until I return."

She gestured at the soldiers standing just beyond the altercation. "Return to your duty." They turned and scurried back to the armory doors. She turned on her heel, slipped between the half open doors and was gone.

Thomas sank to the ground, staring after her. "Who *is* she?" he murmured with dread. He'd never seen anyone use magic before.

§ § §

Thomas jerked in surprise when the doors slammed open and thudded against the walls on either side of the salle doorway. He jumped to his feet, leaving the sword and scabbard lying on the floor.

His father, but an aspect of his father he'd never seen before, strode into the hall. Two guards followed close behind him.

The Duke's face was flushed, filled with controlled fury. His bearded jaw was clenched, eyes narrowed, lips thin. The black and red tattoo of a Dragon that rode his arm, curled up his neck and over his shoulder, seemed to writhe. His left hand gripped the pommel of the sword at his side with white knuckles. Lady Aeden glided in his wake like a sleek mountain lion.

Garan, still lying on the floor as if tied to it, swallowed audibly. Eyes wide, he began to struggle to rise. Aeden looked at him, releasing her spell with a wave of her hand. He scrambled to his feet.

"Boy, where do you come from?" rumbled Duke Tom.

"Sir, I am from North Meall. My father is Earl Tildon," muttered Garan, staring at the ground.

"And your father has called me a - I believe you said - a jumped up captain from the guard? And said that my son is nothing?" the Duke snarled through clenched teeth. "Puppies usually repeat what they've heard."

Garan started to tremble.

"Lord, I didn't mean to insult you or your son," he choked out.

"Then you should have kept your mouth shut," roared the Duke. "Gather your gear. You leave under guard within the candlemark. I'll not harbor a snake in the middle of my Keep. Go. Now!"

The guards grabbed Garan by either arm and shoved him quickly out of sight through the doors.

Thomas stood stunned. The dust in the air tickled his throat and irritated his eyes, making tears run. *Of course. That was it. The dust.* He wiped his eyes with the backs of his hands, bent and picked up the sword and scabbard.

His father turned to him. "Thomas, you are first born and my heir. You need fear no one. While your mother and I are gone, Lady Aeden will be your teacher in all things having to do with weapons and tactics. You will learn states-craft and strategy with Gregory. I've been putting this off, waiting until you were older and I had more time. I just ran out of it." He ran his hand distractedly through his hair. "I thought I'd kept you safe from danger." He shook his head, his lips thin with regret. "Well, it's done."

Thomas stared in shock at this stranger who inhabited his father's body. Slowly joy crept in. He could hardly contain it. He felt like jumping in the air and running around the hall. He'd not known that his father cared.

"Thank you, Father. I promise I'll work hard."

The Duke reached out and clasped Thomas by the shoulder. Giving it a little shake, he said, "Come. Let's put the sword away. There's much to be done before we leave and you can help."

Chapter 2

Thomas and Owen, his younger brother, picked up the next boxes of supplies stacked in the hallway. They hurried down the stairs and handed the boxes to the skullies standing at the bottom. The skullies carried them to the wagons waiting outside. Thomas wiped the sweat from his face with his hands and then wiped them on his tunic.

The two boys carried load after load down to the wagons, working the rest of the afternoon in the sweltering heat and into the cooling breezes of the evening. Thomas's sister, Breanna, worked with her mother, putting the small things Lady Jenni would need into bags and then into boxes.

Duchess Jenni stuck her head out of her bower and shouted, "Thomas, come here. I need you." She looked down the hall at him with tired brown eyes, a crooked smile and hands on her hips as she stepped into the hallway. She was dressed in old grey trousers, a blue shirt that had seen better days and a pair of very well broken-in black boots. Her face was covered with sweat and dust from moving trunks and boxes. Her long dark brown hair was braided down her back, almost to her hips.

She'd filled a traveling trunk with all the clothing she'd need for this hurried trip to the seat of the kingdom. She struggled to move it once it was packed, and found that she could not.

Thomas was taking a break, leaning against the wall at the top of the stairs, tired from the many trips up and down. He took a deep breath, put his hands on his lower back and arched backwards. Every disc in his spine cracked. He twisted slowly from side to side, then sprinted down the hall and grabbed the door frame, swinging around it into his mother's bower. His stomach rumbled with hunger.

"Sorry, Mother," he said as he grinned. "I've had nothing to eat since mid-meal." He grabbed the side handle of the trunk she had finished packing and pulled it into the hallway.

Laughing, she patted him on the back. "Let's gather everyone up and go see what there is for dinner. I'm hungry, too." She raised her voice. "Tom, Owen, Breanna. Let's have some dinner."

Lord Tom walked out of the bedroom. "Good idea," he said to Lady Jenni.

Breanna, short and sturdy with red-gold hair braided down her back and smudges of dust framing her green eyes, walked out of the bower to stand behind her mother. Owen, taller than Breanna but still shorter than his brother, ran up the stairs from his latest trip down, brushing his sweaty dark brown hair out of his blue eyes.

His father smiled at Thomas. "Come on. Let's make this trip down count before we eat." He grabbed one of the side handles and Thomas grabbed the other. They walked to the stairway and Thomas turned and started down the stairs backwards, his father pulling back against the weight of the trunk and taking one step at a time. Once at the bottom, they hauled the trunk to the doorway leading to the forecourt and set it on the floor. The stablemen waiting there lifted the trunk and carried it down the stairs to the wagon slowly filling as supplies were loaded.

The others followed the Duke and Thomas down the stairs.

"Thank you, Thomas. That was well done. I can't believe you've grown so strong." Lady Jenni reached up and gripped his arm, rubbing lightly up and down. "Look at you. When did you get so tall? Taller than I am." She shook her head.

They made their way to their places at the head table as skullies brought food and drink and placed it in front of them. They started eating as soon as they dished the food onto their plates. Breanna was so tired she fell asleep in her chair, her head pillowed on her arm resting on the table next to her plate.

As soon as he finished eating, Duke Tom pushed back from the table and stood. He gently lifted Breanna into his arms and carried her off to bed.

The boys and Lady Jenni finished the last of the cinnamon apples they had been served for dessert and started back to work.

Everything was finally packed and loaded. The wagons stood ready for the horses and drivers that would accompany the Duke and Duchess to the capital.

"Go to bed now, Thomas," the duchess murmured to her son as they stood in the great hall. "You've been a tremendous help. Go on now." She patted him on the back.

Thomas gave her a hug good night and then trudged up the stairs to his room.

Muscles he didn't know he had protested as he grabbed the bottom of his tunic and pulled it over his head. He stripped off the remainder of his clothing, leaving it where it landed, fell into his bed and was instantly asleep in the very early candlemarks of the morning.

$§ § §$

At mid-morning the next day, the Duke called Thomas to him in the forecourt as he checked the saddle and bridle on both his and the Duchess's warhorses. He tightened the girth on his big red roan. The horse squealed and kicked. Both the Duke and Duchess refused to ride in their carriage, wanting the freedom and maneuverability of being ahorse.

"Pay attention to Lady Aeden and Gregory. Gregory has forgotten strategy that I'm still learning. That's why I appointed him as my seneschal. He can help you with any problems. Captain Mathin is in charge of defenses for the Keep, but he'll be bringing you in to council for instruction. Listen to him as well. Continue your lessons."

Thomas nodded. "Yes sir."

"It will take us at least three weeks to reach Cathair Ri. I expect we'll be gone until spring, maybe late winter at the earliest.

Remember, you are my heir. Look after your brother and sister. Watch your back."

The Duke turned to him and pulled him into a rough hug. He released Thomas, turned and put his left boot into the stirrup and swung into his saddle. Duchess Jenni strode out of the Keep doors, pulling a pair of riding gloves over her long fingered hands. She descended the stairs and took the reins of her destrier from the groom. Turning to Thomas, she hugged him tight. "Stay safe," she whispered huskily in his ear. She gathered the horse's reins and mounted, as graceful as her husband. The horses tossed their heads and danced across the cobbles. They were firmly checked back into a sidling walk and then halted by both riders next to Thomas.

His mother leaned down and ruffled his hair. "See you soon," she said. She smiled and reined her horse around to follow the Duke to the head of the column.

Thomas turned and took the stairs two at a time to the top of the staircase that fronted the doors into Dragon Tower, the better to watch the cavalcade get under way.

Owen and Breanna waved from their second story balcony. "Goodbye, Father. Goodbye, Mother. Ride safe," they shouted as loudly as they could down at the assembly. They were not allowed into the forecourt with so many horses, men and confusion.

The Duke and Duchess, thirty guards and the supply wagons rumbled into motion. They rolled through the gates and were on their way. The Duke and Duchess raised their arms in farewell to those left behind.

$ $ $

Thomas hurried across the forecourt and ran up the stairs to the rampart on top of the wall surrounding the central towers of Red Dragon's Keep. He watched until he could no longer see even their dust trail. Fear and sorrow at their departure battled with joy at the changes in his life.

He looked down over the rampart walls to the dry moat surrounding the Keep. The dark grey granite walls rose three stories above the ground at this point. Thomas hoped they were tall enough if war with Demons was coming.

The Keep rose above a hanging valley reached by a switch-back road on the side of Slieve Geal, the Shining Mountain. Songs were sung of the last battle of the last war with the Ciardha Demons fought on its flanks. Red Dragon's Keep guarded the farthest north of the four passes that cut through the Dragon Spine Mountains rising north to south, forming a backbone for Ard An Tir. The territory that the Duke controlled was the largest in Ard Ri, covering an area ten days ride in any direction from the Keep.

A large walled town overflowing with shops and cottages filled the valley to the west of the Tower. Villagers bringing produce, meat and other goods from the countryside hurried along the streets and set up shop on almost every corner. A livestock market claimed space on the side of the town furthest from the Dragon Tower. Thomas watched a cloud of dust billow into the air as cattle were driven into corrals maintained for that purpose. The noise of the town echoed against the walls of the Keep.

A sinking feeling of panic gripped his stomach and dread caught his breath. *What am I going to do? I don't know anything about running the duchy.* He thought about what his father had said. Captain Mathin, Gregory and Lady Aeden were going to teach him. It would be all right.

He looked along the length of the rampart, marking the soldiers pacing its length to the watchtowers on either end. Two sentries were stationed at the crenellations midway on the parapet, keeping watch.

Thomas turned and looked up the walls of the central tower of the Keep. They rose three stories higher, tall and strong. The image of a red winged Dragon laid in stone stretched its length up the eastern side of the Dragon Tower wall.

The sun was rising noon when he turned and slowly walked down the rampart stairs and made his way across the forecourt. This was the first time that he and his brother and sister had ever been left alone at Red Dragon's Keep. Owen and Breanna met him as he climbed the stairs into the Dragon Tower.

"What did Father say to you?" asked Owen as they walked across the main hall and up the stairs toward their rooms. He was thirteen, stocky with dark brown hair and blue eyes. The top of his head just reached Thomas's chin.

"Hurry up. We need to change for mid-meal," Breanna said, as she rushed after them, turning into the family corridor. She wore dirt-stained brown leggings and a cream tunic that was too small. Her red-blond hair was braided down her back. She'd been out with the horses in the stable before the cavalcade left. Blue eyes squinted at Thomas. Her eleven years made her bossy.

Thomas stopped in the middle of the hall. "Father told me I needed to take care of both of you. I'm going to be working with Lady Aeden, Gregory and Captain Mathin, learning weapons and strategy. I really need your help."

Owens' and Breanna's eyes went round with surprise.

"Father is letting you learn to fight? Why not me?" Owen shrilled.

"Cause you're not big enough yet," giggled Breanna.

"How about I ask Lady Aeden to let you train too, Owen?" Thomas answered with a grin.

"Yes," Owen shouted and pumped his fist in the air.

"Can I learn strategy with you?" asked Breanna.

"I can ask," Thomas said with a smile for her.

"Hurry up. We're going to be late." Breanna pushed past the boys and ran to her room.

Chapter 3

The weather had turned overnight and frost had nipped the valley. The day would be hot later but right now it was chilly. Lady Aeden sought out Thomas in the great hall at breakfast the next morning.

He'd just started his meal when she approached the high table.

"My Lord, I've something to discuss with you in the Solar when you're finished, if you please. It has to do with the defense of Red Dragon's Keep. Will you meet me there in half a candlemark?"

"Of course, Lady Aeden," he responded. "Could you let Gregory know where I'll be? I'm supposed to meet with him about battle strategy."

"I'll tell him, my Lord. I'll meet you in the Solar."
She turned and walked back toward Gregory's office.

Half a candlemark later Thomas climbed the stairs to the top of the main tower and the Solar. The bright light from windows around the entire room allowed the women of the Keep to work on sewing and embroidery, spinning and weaving. Material, trim, buttons and thread were stacked on the shelves that rose between the windows. A loom sat ready for use and a quilting frame held a quilt that waited for the needles of his mother's ladies. With his mother gone, her ladies had taken the day to do personal errands.

Lady Aeden stood looking out of the tower window that faced east. Her face wore a troubled frown. She turned as she heard Thomas enter the room.

"What is it, my Lady?"

"I'm not sure. I felt something when I looked out the window, but what it is I don't know." She shrugged her shoulders. "We'll know if something is amiss soon enough."

She moved to one of the upholstered chairs next to the fireplace centered between the windows on the north side. "Come. Sit. I want to talk to you about magic."

Thomas jerked back in surprise and concern. He frowned and his head tilted in query. Magery was practiced openly by very few. Those who had no magic distrusted those who did. Suspicion that a person could read thoughts or control another with magic often created fear. Fear could lead to murder of the magic wielder, so most kept quiet if they did have the power. He moved to sit in the chair across from her.

"Lady, why do you want to talk to me about it? I have no magic."

Aeden tilted her head and quietly gazed at him. The silence grew uncomfortable.

Thomas shifted uneasily in the chair. "I'm sorry," he hazarded, not knowing what he had done wrong.

"I can feel the magic in you, Thomas. You need to train it just like you will be training your body in the use of weapons."

"I have magic?" Thomas asked in amazement. "I've never felt any magic. I don't even know what it is."

"Yes, you do. Everyone has some magic in them." She looked at Thomas then gave a shrug.

"The first thing to do is learn to center your-self and create a shield. Close your eyes and think about nothing. Feel the flow of energy in your gut."

Thomas did as she asked. He closed his eyes and quieted his thoughts, something he wasn't used to doing. At first, he felt nothing as random thoughts fired through his mind. As he waited, he thought that he could feel the energy centered right under his heart.

"Can you feel it?"

Thomas nodded. "I think so."

"That's the energy at the core of your being. When you are calm and centered, think about extending that energy through your body and down through your feet like roots, deep into the earth. It will anchor you and give you access to the power of earth. Try it now."

Thomas pictured a ball of energy centered at his stomach. He waited and felt warmth start to grow. His eyes flew open and he looked at Aeden in astonishment. The warmth faded.

"*That* is your ki. Try again."

He closed his eyes and pictured the energy in his mind's eye. As the warmth grew, he pictured roots extending from it into the earth far below. Power slowly grew until he fairly vibrated with it.

"Now, slowly release the energy and let it drain back into the earth. Feel the calmness of that release."

Thomas did as she instructed, feeling the energy drain away. He opened his eyes and looked at her with a little fear. "What can I do with that energy? I felt like I was buzzing with it."

"You can extend that energy to others, make objects move, hold things immobile as I did with Garan. There are many things you can do. The most important thing to learn right now is control: summoning and releasing and shielding.

You also need to pay attention when the power starts to fail. That is the signal to release it and rest. All magic demands a price. That price for us is death if we use the power to total exhaustion! You must eat something soon after using it. Food helps replenish your power, both physically and mentally. Now, call the power again and hold it steady."

Thomas did so. He could feel it wavering as he tried to do what she asked.

"Think of a shield of air standing between you and the world."

Thomas concentrated and built a wall of air around him. It felt heavy and dense. He lost his concentration and the shield wavered and snapped away.

Frustrated, he leaned forward in his chair and tried again. This time the shield didn't even form. Bewildered, he looked at Aeden. She turned her head and looked at him steadily.

"What am I doing wrong," he asked in exasperation.

"How calm are you?" she asked.

Chagrined, he closed his eyes and calmed his mind and heartbeat.

Again he formed a picture in his mind of a shield around him. As the shield grew, he began to feel like he couldn't breathe. He panicked and released the power all at once.

It surged back into him. Pain racked his body as his back arched and he drew in a huge breath. The pain slowly subsided.

"What was that?" he exclaimed.

"You built a very tight shield," Aeden smiled. "And, that's what happens when you release the power too quickly. Control is everything. Magic is very literal. You want to build a shield that is loose enough to allow air through but still dense enough to protect you."

"Let's try something else. Focus your energy into a ball of light on your hand. Like this."

Aeden held out her hand, centered herself and slowly allowed her energy to manifest as a ball of magelight on her hand so that Thomas could follow the steps. She gently sent it floating over their heads.

"Could you feel what I did, Thomas?"

"Yes, I did. I felt everything. Let me try."

Thomas centered himself, held out his hand and squinted his eyes, his lips pressed tight in concentration, as he attempted to create magelight. A small ball of fitfully flickering light appeared above his hand.

He laughed in excitement. The light winked out of existence.

Aeden smiled.

"Very good. Now, let's create a shield that lets you breathe."

$ $ $

Thomas's eyes drooped as he shoved the needle through the material of his torn tunic. He jerked himself awake and yawned mightily, stretching his arms over his head until his spine cracked. He had plans for the night even though all he wanted to do was sleep. Using magic was hard work.

He kept himself awake mending his ripped trousers. His mother had insisted he learn how to take care of his own clothing. As soon as that chore was done, he folded the mended clothes and placed them in his trunk at the foot of the bed. He walked to his door and quietly pulled it open, checking for any noise or movement. He heard only the sounds that night brought to the Keep: the last clatter from the kitchen echoing up the stairwell, the scuff of boots as the guards patrolled corridors.

Closing the door, he dropped an iron pin through the lock hasp. He walked over to the wall next to the wardrobe that stood to the left of the fireplace facing his bed. The room was paneled with dark wood half way up the stone wall. Tapestries showing battles from Red Dragon's Keep history hung from the ceiling to the paneling. They blocked out the chill radiating from the stone. Firelight flickered on the wall hangings, making the woven figures seem to move.

He lifted the edge of the tapestry and tapped on the upper left corner of the first stone block above the paneling. He reached down and pushed on the lower right corner of the paneling next to the wardrobe. Finally he pushed down on the edge of the panel right at elbow height above the right corner.

There was a click, and a crack appeared in the paneling and stone block. Thomas pushed on the crack and the stone wall swept into a passage that yawned into darkness to the left and the right.

He'd found the opening by accident last Yule's eve, pretending to be a thief looking for hidden treasure. He'd heard wild rumors all his life about secret passages in the Tower.

Tapping, tugging, shoving and imagining had taken up candlemarks of his time. He was shocked when the hidden door opened and he'd almost fallen through into the dusty passage. He'd felt along the edges of the door for the locking mechanism and jammed it with a scrap he tore from one of his worn tunics ready to be turned into rags.

Figuring out the pattern to push again had taken many more candlemarks. Once he'd found it by listening for the click of the released lock, he'd written down the combination on a scrap of paper and hidden it behind the lining in the trunk holding his clothes.

Exploring the passages that connected to this one opened a whole new way to keep track of what was going on in his father's duchy.

He listened in at his father's council meetings and to Captain Mathin and Gregory as they discussed the Keep and its defense and maintenance.

He'd told no one about his discovery. It was his delicious secret.

Thomas lit a small lantern. He put on his soft-soled boots and stepped into the darkness to the left. He walked into cobwebs that had grown there since he'd last gone exploring. He wiped them from his face in disgust. He raised his arm in front of his head to keep them away, and started down the passage again.

Thomas had listened shamelessly to Gregory telling Captain Mathin about a meeting in his office with returning scouts after the Tower settled for the night. The scouts were returning from a mission to check on reports of Demon attacks. Thomas wanted desperately to hear that report.

He hurried along the corridor, trying not to scuff his feet. He came to the set of narrow stairs that descended to the first floor and took them down two at a time.

The passage passed to the left of Gregory's office behind the fireplace. The fire heated the brick and kept the dark stone corridor pleasantly warm.

He shuttered the lantern and set it on the floor after putting his hand on one of the bricks to the side of the fireplace. The passageway was plunged into darkness. Thomas slowly pulled the loose brick where his hand rested out of its home. He carefully set it next to the lantern at his feet. He breathed through his mouth so as not to make a sound.

He put his eyes to the gap left by the removal of the brick. He could see dimly through the tapestry hanging on the other side of the wall. More importantly, he was in time and he could hear.

Gregory sat behind his desk. Darkness pressed against the tall windows that reflected the room. Two scouts pushed through the door into the office. They wore dark brown tunics and trousers covered by oilcloth capes beaded with moisture. Both slumped wearily.

"Hang your capes behind the door." Gregory gestured toward the back of the door into the room.

The scouts pulled them off and hung them on the hooks mounted there.

"Sit before you fall," Gregory ordered.

They gratefully walked over and collapsed into the two chairs sitting in front of his desk.

"What did you see?" Gregory asked as he got up, came around to the corner of the desk closest to the fireplace and half sat on it.

"The Steadings to the south and west are gone," the first scout replied, shaking his head. "Everyone and everything is dead. Babes and mothers, fathers, children, oldsters, everyone. We watched as they slaughtered all of the farm animals and burned all of the buildings. There was nothing we could do.

There is something traveling with the Demons that waits until all living things have been turned or killed and it releases a gas that ignites when it reaches one of the fires burning in the houses. The fires spread from there."

The second scout continued, "We were attacked on the way back to the Keep by humans that the Ciardha twisted somehow. I've never seen anything like them. They look vaguely like us but there is nothing human left in them. They 'feel' empty. Their eyes burn red, just as the Demons do. They attacked as soon as they saw us. They don't die easy. They just keep attacking until their head is taken." He began to shudder.

Gregory stood quickly and moved to a table set against the wall between bookcases. It held a jug and glasses. Thomas could smell the mead that filled the jug. Gregory poured a glass for each scout and himself and carried them back to the exhausted men. They took the glasses gratefully and downed the drink in several gulps.

Gregory waved toward the table. "Serve yourselves." Neither man left his seat.

"Could you tell how many had been 'twisted' from the Steadings you saw? Are they traveling with the Demons or are they being 'twisted' and then let loose on us?"

"Sir, I couldn't tell." The first scout spoke slowly. The scouts glanced at each other then looked back at Gregory. "Truthfully, once they are changed it's really difficult to know who they are. Their faces elongate and so do their teeth and nails. Their eyes turn red. They seem to gain strength too. They look like another form of Demon. I think most are turned loose by their 'masters' to hunt and kill. Some stayed with the Demon horde. Even weirder, not all of the humans are 'twisted'." The first scout shook his head in disbelief.

"Is there anything else that you can recall?" asked Gregory.

"I'm sure there's more," said the first scout. "I'm so tired I can hardly think. Maybe in the morning."

"Right," said Gregory with a sigh. "Get some rest and then see me in the morning after breakfast. We'll want to make a record of this."

The scouts left the room, grabbing their much drier capes from the back of the door on their way out.

Gregory sat at his desk, his elbows on its cluttered surface and fingers steepled in front of his mouth. With another sigh and shake of his head he rose, took the candlestick on his desk in hand and left the room, pulling the door shut after him.

Thomas unshuttered the lantern at his feet. He didn't want to think about the scouts' report yet. He'd wait until he was back in his room.

He carefully replaced the brick he had removed. He had a sneaking hunch that he wouldn't be getting much sleep for the rest of the night.

He soft-footed his way back along the passage to his room and made sure that the secret panel was closed and locked after he went through. He twitched the tapestry to make sure the line of the door was hidden.

The fire snapped and sparked as he put another log on it. He walked over to unlock his door into the main corridor. It would never do to keep it locked and not let his chamberlain have access in the morning.

Questions tumbled over thoughts as he changed into his nightclothes. Nothing he had read told of Demons turning humans into monsters.

Why and how? How many had been twisted? Would they be facing an army of the 'Twisted'? He'd already named them in his mind.

He crawled into bed and tried to think about riding in battle maneuvers.

Anything to shut off his questions.

Chapter 4

Deep purple shadows slowly lengthened across the cart path that Marta Haloran trudged along toward the Steading. The path followed the river as best it could, sometimes close, sometimes avoiding dense copses of trees or marshy areas filled with mud and cattails along the riverbanks.

The back of her coarse brown skirt was drawn up between her legs and through her belt in the front, keeping it out of her way. The wooden yoke she carried across her shoulders was heavy. Baskets on either end of the yoke held the things she'd bought in the village. The treats, spices and notions that the Steading couldn't produce had taken longer to buy than she'd allowed for.

She wished she'd been able to ride one of the horses into the village, but they were all in use clearing the fields of hay for the coming winter. She tried to move at an even pace so that the baskets didn't swing too hard, yet she also hurried as quickly as she could. Everyone knew there were Demons roaming from sunset to sunrise.

The westering sun sank behind the mountain. It disappeared and the temperature dropped. A chill crept up Marta's spine. She was a half a mile from home. She hoped that she could reach it quickly.

The grey river on her right swirled and gurgled against its bank. Dark woods on her left seemed to lean closer over the path, leafless branches trying to reach for her burden. Something rustled in the depths of the trees. Branches snapped as a heavy body pushed through them. She looked fearfully into the deepening gloom.

She began to jog toward home. The path swung away from the river. The baskets swung wildly with each jarring step.

Panting and grunting, snapping and breaking of brush and small trees on both sides of the path sounded behind her. She *must not* look. She gasped for breath. Her heart thundered in her chest. Fear-sweat streamed down her face. A grunting cough sounded right behind her. She dropped the yoke and took off running. Baskets shattered, releasing food and goods across the path.

She burst out of the trees into the meadow that fronted her family's Steading. Fear gripped her muscles as she tried to run faster. Standing at the gate through the wooden walls of the Steading, her father and two brothers held lit torches against the gathering darkness. They gripped old swords and spears kept from the last war, other weapons standing sentinel behind them, thrust into the ground within easy reach.

Marta heard grunting and heavy panting closing in behind her. The thud of many feet shook the ground.

"Run, Marta! Run!" screamed her father.

She shrieked voicelessly in fear as she hurtled toward the gate.

Her brother drew back his arm and launched the spear that he held toward her. It flew over her right shoulder. A howl sounded almost in her ear. She ducked away and found a little extra speed.

She raced toward her father. As she reached him, she grabbed his left arm. She used him as a pivot, swung around and grabbed the spear that stood upright behind her brother. Arrows rained down on the Demons from behind the palisade walls, loosed by the men and women on the rampart.

The Demon horrors that they faced stopped to eat the thrashing, dying members of their horde. Course grey hair obscured loose black skin covering hunched bodies the size of ponies. Black claws sprouted from all four feet. Long muzzles filled with serrated teeth snapped and tore at the screaming, dying Demons. Upright ears projected from large round heads. Enormous deep red eyes glistened, pupils huge in the twilight. There were at least twelve left standing.

Feeding done, the Demons turned toward Marta and her father and brothers. Her father hissed, "Back, back into the palisade. Quick, don't turn around, just step back."

The Demons milled in a hideous hissing growling mass, darting forward, trying to get behind them. The defenders backed through the partially open gate, stabbing at the Demons as they tried to slip under the spears and swords to get at the meat they craved.

Marta's mother and brothers heaved the gate closed as her granda slammed the crossbar into its brackets. Bodies thudded again and again against the gate, making the wood flex and groan.

"Up on the rampart. Start the fireballs," her father barked. The holders desperately obeyed their Steader as quickly as they could.

Everyone in the Steading still on the ground ran up on the rampart and grabbed the pitch-soaked balls mounted on arrows. The balls were touched to braziers kept lit for the purpose and burst into flame.

Shooting down on the Demon beasts, the pitch-covered balls stuck to skin and burned into flesh. Once ignited, the Demons could not put out the fires.

They broke off their attack and threw themselves to the ground, rolling and spinning, trying to dislodge the burning pitch. They fled shrieking, back into the woods, setting small brush fires as they ran. Rain would soon douse the fires.

With a sob, Marta put her back to the palisade wall and slid down. *How could they survive another attack? How could they survive?*

Marta's mother, Raina, dropped down beside her. She put her arms around Marta's shoulders and hugged her hard.

"I thought we'd lost you. We can't stay here any longer. We're leaving tomorrow morning at sunrise. Put together your journey pack as quick as you can and help

Granda with his. We need as much food as we can carry. We're going to Red Dragon's Keep."

"Mama, what are those things? Have you ever seen anything like them before?"

"I've never seen them, but I remember stories from the Great War." Raina shuddered.

Chapter 5

Thomas lifted his heavy wooden practice sword into first position.

"Remember, Thomas, you must move and move and move. Never stand still. Use the flat of your sword to set aside the blows from the other sword. Let the enemy's sword slide along the flat of your blade," murmured Lady Aeden.

"As his sword slides down your blade, twist it away from you and cut opposite to his strike."

She demonstrated the move. "Watch your opponent's chest. Tightening there tells you when and where he will attack. Do not block; attack."

Thomas swung his wooden sword up across his body and back down to his side.

Lady Aeden started his training two days after his parents left for the capital. The staff sergeant in charge of the squires roused him out of bed before dawn. He'd set Thomas to training with the squires who served the officers of the Keep. At first, running for miles each morning along the roads that met at the Keep sent him to the baths in agony, his legs cramping and his body aching. As his body hardened, the pain grew less and he adjusted to the heavy work.

Captain Mathin requested Thomas as his squire. Every day, as soon as training with the other squires was over, he hurried through his bath then trotted to Captain Mathin's quarters where he oiled the officer's chain-mail armor, vambraces and chausses and sharpened his sword. He dreamed of his own armor as he labored.

"Thomas, focus," Aeden corrected him sharply. She brought her sword into the next position, waiting for Thomas to bring his sword up and across. Fortunately for his peace of mind, there were no other trainees present who might note his awkward progress. Dust stirred up by his movements across the wooden planks covering the sand-filled pit in the center of the salle floated in the streams of sunlight falling through the clerestory windows. Huge mirrors, used to check body alignment and position in the exercises, were mounted on the west wall.

Thomas completed the set of eight moves that he had been taught as Aeden flowed in the corresponding pattern. By the end of the set, his wrists, arms and hands felt as weak as wet noodles. He'd been working on this exercise for over a candlemark. Aeden neatly twisted the sword from his hand.

"Move your feet in the correct pattern as well," said Aeden sternly.

She sheathed her sword.

"Come; let's set you at the pells today to bring the patterns together."

Gratefully, Thomas picked up and sheathed his sword, shaking out his wrists. He walked with her to the door on the west wall next to the mirrors. They stepped out of the salle into a brisk bright afternoon. They followed the stone walk from the salle to the outdoor arena set between the stables and storage buildings. All of the officers, squires and men-at-arms practiced individual and group movements there. At the end of the arena, four head-high thick posts, called pells, had been buried in the earth as deep as they were tall.

"Now, use the pattern against the pell. As you hit it, shift your weight and return with the opposite strike." Aeden folded her arms across her chest and stood back to watch.

Thomas took his place in front of the pell and readied his arms, extending his practice sword down and away from his body. He brought it up and hit the pell at throat height. The sword bounced off the pell and he moved with its trajectory and brought it around to hit the other side. His hands and arms moved in the pattern and his feet followed. Sweat covered him from head to toe as he spun and hit again and again. He grinned maniacally. On his last strike, the sword hit at the wrong angle and bounced back against his thigh. He shook his head in resignation.

"Again," Aeden commanded.

After two more repetitions, his movements had slowed to a snail's pace, but every blow was accurate. He came to the end of the pattern and raised his sword in triumph.

"Ha. I did it," he exclaimed.

Lady Aeden smiled. "Of course you did. You've been training hard. A little more time on the pells and you can start sparring with the other squires. You're doing very well. Have you been practicing with Maccon and Stefan?"

"I have, my Lady. We've become good friends since Garan left." He frowned. "It's funny. As soon as he left, almost everyone else started treating me like a person." Thomas sheathed his practice sword in its scabbard hanging at his left hip. He wiped his sweating face with the bottom of his shirt as he and Aeden walked toward the trough of water at the side of the arena. He dunked his head completely in the trough and swung up quickly, water arching as he shook his head. The cool water felt good.

Lady Aeden chuckled. "Garan was a troublemaker, that's for sure. Time for your lessons with Captain Mathin. How are they progressing?" she asked.

"They're going well, I think." Thomas wiped the water off of his face with his hands. "We're covering the last Demon war - what worked and didn't work for the allies. It's fascinating. The Ciardha Demons tried again and again to seize the initiative and never could. We can't figure out why, but I have a feeling that is the most important point." Thomas frowned in thought. "Have you heard anything that might bear on it?"

"No, but I'll ask around and look into it. Perhaps others will know," Aeden answered. They stopped at the door to the salle.

"Lady Aeden, I promised my brother that I would ask if he could start training, too. He's been nagging at me to ask you since Father left. He may be small for his age, but he should know how to fight just like I need to know. He's growing really fast. Could he maybe attend training classes for the youngest squires?"

Lady Aeden crossed her arms, a frown lowering her brows. "Let me talk with Captain Mathin and Gregory. I agree that he should be trained, and perhaps Breanna as well, at least in knife work. It's a good thought, Thomas. Go on." She smiled and waved toward the tower. "Captain Mathin is waiting."

With a broad grin and a flip of his wet blond hair out of his eyes, Thomas took off at a jog for his next lessons.

$ $ $

"Captain Mathin, I don't understand why the King's council refused to spend the money for more soldiers. It only makes sense to be prepared for whatever might happen."

Thomas shook his head, bewildered by what he had read in the records of the kingdom and Red Dragon's Keep. "The town councils don't want to pay for more soldiers, just like the king's council. I understand it takes money from everyone, but we need more soldiers now," he exclaimed. "War is coming and we need to get ready."

He and Captain Mathin waited for Gregory in the Duke's Library. Thomas met with them there each day for his lessons on tactics and strategy.

The Library was located in the southwest side of the Tower, catching both morning and afternoon light from the windows around the room. It took up the entire fourth floor. Permanent records of the Keep and surrounding lands were kept there as well as the extremely rare and valuable books that the Arach family had collected for generations. Thomas and his siblings, as well as other highborn trainees, were given lessons in this room.

Tall broad windows facing south allowed in as much light as possible. Heavy thick wooden shutters were folded back against the walls on either side of the windows, ready to bar the openings in case of attack.

Bookshelves lined the room on three sides. Captain Mathin leaned against one of them, his arms folded across his chest. He tilted his head to the side in interest. "Where did you hear that?"

Thomas knew that he had surprised Captain Mathin more than once with information he had gleaned from listening around the Keep and village and especially from his time spent listening in the secret passageways.

He looked everywhere but at the captain. Thomas didn't want to tell him about the corridor behind the great hall. He hung his head and replied, "I've listened to you and Father and Gregory discussing strategy and tactics after dinner. I've paid attention to the soldiers whenever I'm down in the village. I know I was supposed to be doing other things but I couldn't help myself."

"So how do you think we can convince the town councils that we need more soldiers?"

Thomas leaned his elbow on the table and cupped his chin in his hand. "What if we sent out the news from the dispatches we've received with the town criers to every village in the duchy?" Thomas spoke hesitantly.

"Do you think that might make the villagers panic?"

Thomas frowned. He could see the solution but didn't know how to say it. He tried anyway. "If everyone knows what's happening, maybe we can get them to help us. Nobody out there knows the truth, because we don't tell them. They already know something's wrong, and I've heard the wildest rumors down in town. This will give them information instead of rumors. Those on the village and town councils will hear the news and maybe recognize that we all better get ready."

Captain Mathin stroked his beard as he gazed out the windows as if weighing Thomas's idea. "It just might work," he murmured, almost to himself. They turned toward the door as it opened to reveal the seneschal.

"Gregory, Thomas has a good idea. What do you think about this?"

Chapter 6

"Thomas, pick a quarterstaff that's as tall as you are. Yes, that's the right size. Stefan, Maccon, you do the same."

It was cool in the salle. Thomas pulled a quarterstaff from its rack next to the training floor, grounded its butt and ran his hand up the polished wood, just to feel its satin smoothness.

The instructor for the training class was an older man, hunch-backed, with a mane of white hair floating wildly around his head. His white mustache blended into his beard that ended at mid-belly. He leaned heavily on a quarterstaff that was a third again taller than he was. He had been training squires for Duke Arach for many, many years. He walked with a heavy limp. His leg had been sliced with a pike and had healed badly.

"Take your places on the floor," he said quietly.

The three squires lined up at the center of the floor.

"Stefan and Thomas, pair off. Maccon, you and I will practice together."

Stefan and Thomas took their positions facing each other, quarterstaffs held horizontally at waist height, hands shoulder-width apart. Stefan lashed out towards Thomas with the left butt of his staff. Thomas blocked the blow and followed through with a strike towards Stefan's stomach. Stefan sprang back and brought his staff down towards Thomas's leg. He caught him behind the knee and jerked forward, tumbling Thomas to the ground.

"Ha," shouted Thomas as he fell. "Good one, Stefan." He jumped back to his feet.

The old man stood waiting for Maccon to strike. Hesitantly, Maccon brought his staff up towards the outside edge of the weapons-master's staff. With a blur, the old man swung his staff around his head and straight toward Maccon. With a shout of fear, Maccon ducked and instinctively threw up his staff. The old man's move knocked the staff from Maccon's hands. The old man reversed his staff and thrust again toward Maccon, the butt of his staff stopping an inch from Maccon's forehead.

"That won't do, Maccon. Again."

Maccon retrieved his staff with a shake of his head. "I'll never get this, Master," he groaned.

The old man chuckled. "Yes, you will. I assure you that you will learn. We will take each position slowly until you have the pattern down precisely."

As soon as Maccon returned to his starting position, the old man moved with him through the pattern, again and again and again. By the eighth repetition, Maccon was exhausted, but he knew the pattern.

"Rest," said the old man. He turned and regarded Stefan and Thomas.

Those two had been steadily working through the forms. The padded ends of the training quarterstaffs provided at least some protection from broken bones, bruises, and even killing strokes. Thomas had a black eye from not moving fast enough to block a blow to his face. Stefan limped badly on a bruised leg from a sweep by Thomas.

"Rest," the old man told them.

Quarterstaff butts thudded against the floor and the squires leaned on them gratefully.

"You've done well. Return the equipment to its place and go to your next lessons," the old man dismissed them. "I'll see you tomorrow."

"Those were some good moves, Stefan," Thomas said as the three boys walked to the weapons rack. "Where did you learn them?"

Stefan huffed a short laugh. "I've been training with staffs since I was little, Lord Thomas. My father said I'd better know how because we didn't have enough money to train me with swords or other weapons. We didn't even have money for leather armor."

Thomas looked at him with new respect. "For not having any other training, you're doing really well, then," he said. "How did you become a squire?" He sneezed violently from the dust in the air raised by their practice.

"Your father knew mine from the last war. When he found out that my father had a son of an age to become a squire, he sent for me. You should have seen my father. He was shocked, and then so proud. My mother started to cry. It was good, and bad. Made me feel happy and sad at the same time."

"I know what you mean. I felt the same way when Father and Mother left," Thomas told him. "What about you, Maccon? What's your story?"

"The town where I grew up sponsored me to your father," Maccon replied. "I've always been good with weapons and horses. There hasn't been anyone else sent as a squire for a very long time. When your father accepted me, the whole town was thrilled. The mayor and council came to see me accepted," he said proudly.

"That's really excellent," Thomas responded with a punch to Maccon's shoulder. "Let's go get mid-meal. I want to hear more. I'll sit with you. Come on." Thomas took off running.

The two boys looked at each other, then took off chasing him with a whoop of laughter.

Chapter 7

Jalyn shook her head as she kneaded the bread dough. Push, fold. Push, fold. The rhythmic movement soothed her mind. The kitchen was sweltering with the heat of the hearth where all of the cooking for the Tower was done.

Nothing was proceeding as it should. There was definitely something blocking her attempts to manipulate that brat, Thomas. She had worked at Red Dragon's Keep for a very long time, waiting for just such opportunities as she'd had in the past months. Even the spells worked against some of the squires seemed to have failed.

She wiped the back of her hand across her sweating forehead. Her gray hair was drawn back into an unattractive bun and dirty tendrils fell down across her forehead. Small, dark brown eyes glared out of an obese face. The fat on the back of her arms jiggled as she moved. She liked to eat.

She hated the Arachs with every fiber of her being. Before the Duke had been confirmed as the holder of Red Dragon's Keep, she'd been the chatelaine and ruled with an iron hand. No one was allowed to shirk under her purview. She'd thought that the Duke's father might have married her after his first wife died.

Now she was the cook. How she wanted to get back at the ones who had taken her former life from her.

She briskly shaped the dough and folded it into its pans. She walked to the bread oven, clumsily skirting the table where apprentices chopped and sliced the meat and vegetables for dinner, ramming her hip into the corner. She slid the pans into the oven and lifted the slate cover over the opening.

Jalyn walked back toward the hearth, stopping to taste the stew that simmered in the pot hung over the kitchen fire. She'd prepared a special dinner for the high table.

Looking around to check if anyone was watching, she slipped a small glass vial from the side pocket in her voluminous skirt. She unstoppered it and poured the contents into the stew. That should send those who thought themselves above her scurrying for the toilet. Maybe it would be enough to kill.

This was the tenth time she had used poison to try to kill the Arachs. None of them had worked. The idiots had complained of odd tastes, but that was all. She could not understand why the poisons hadn't done the job. The Arachs all deserved to die. *I'll just keep trying until something works.*

Her face contorted in a satisfied sneer, she moved back to the dessert table to check her underling's efforts.

She inspected the pastry and peaches, turned and slapped the girl, Clara, across the face. "You've done it again. Burned the crust and put too many peaches in the pie. Do it again," she demanded.

Tears leaked from the pastry cooks eyes. She did not cry out loud. Those who cried were beaten. She bent to start the dessert again.

Jalyn picked up the pie and carried it to the table set at the head of the room, comfortably close to the fire.

She took her seat and began to eat.

Chapter 8

"Thomas, you're ready to choose a sword of your own, one that you can work with until it feels like an extension of your arm," Lady Aeden said as she walked across the salle floor toward him and his partner.

Thomas's practice sword fell away from the guard position as his concentration was broken by Aeden's comment. His sparring partner, Calen, took advantage of his lapse in attention to whack him in the ribs with what felt like the edge of his blade.

"Ow!" Thomas exclaimed. It wasn't the first time that Calen had gotten through his guard and left bruises on his body. He and some of the other squires liked to swagger around the Keep, baiting the girls, kicking the skullies, arrogantly certain that nothing and no one would stop them as long as they didn't act in front of their elders. Garan had been part of that faction.

Maybe Calen and the other squires really are trying to hurt me. He dismissed the thought with a shake of his head. He sheathed his wooden sword.

Lady Aeden laughed. "That's what you get for losing your concentration. Come on. Let's get to the armory. Calen, take Simon as partner."

She and Thomas shared a companionable silence as they walked across the salle, through the doors, turned left and followed the hallway to the older part of the weapons training center. It had been five weeks since he'd started his training. He'd only been allowed as far as the guard's maintenance room where weapons were sharpened, oiled and wooden parts repaired or replaced. Chain-mail links were placed or replaced on leather armor in that room.

A guard sat at a table next to the weapons room double doors, reading records and making notations on them. They stopped in front of the table and Lady Aeden touched her hand to her temple in a casual salute. Another guard stationed in front of the doors came to attention.

"We're here to choose a weapon for Lord Thomas," she told him.

"Yes, my Lady, my Lord," the guard at the table responded, jumping to his feet and giving a short bow.

The guard in front of the doors gave a respectful nod and stepped to the side. Aeden pulled the right-hand door of the room open. She motioned for Thomas to enter first and stepped in behind him. Pulling the door closed, she called mage light to her hand and flicked her wrist, setting it to float above them.

"Try to do the same, Lord Thomas." She gestured at her light. "It's good practice."

Thomas glanced at her, then held out his hand, centered his ki and concentrated his will on creating light. Magelight danced above his fingertips. He moved his hand upward as if tossing a ball and the light soared to the ceiling.

Lady Aeden laughed. "Not quite so vigorously, Lord Thomas. Gently."

He covered his laugh with a cough. He had actually done it right this time.

Lady Aeden crossed her arms over her chest and turned toward the rows and racks of weapons. The smile left her face, and her lips thinned.

Thomas glanced at her then turned to really look at the room and its contents for the first time.

Narrow slit windows at the top of the armory walls allowed dim, dust-filtered light to relieve the gloom. A long wooden table, badly scarred with nicks, scrapes and cuts, but well cleaned, took up the center of the space. The smell of metal, polish and oil permeated the space. The faint coppery hint of old blood underlay it all. The walls were lined with racks holding swords, maces, claymores, falchions, battle axes, and every other weapon of war. Spears, halberds, swordstaffs and poleaxe weapons stood between pegs on floor racks standing along the back wall. The uneven floor of flagstone and walls made of huge stone block radiated the chill of death.

"All of the Arach weapons - won, bought, found, and passed down for generations - are kept here," she said. "Many have come from battle. Some have spells of health or healing, battle frenzy or strategy laid on them. Some are more powerful than that. It is your time to choose." Her last words echoed around the room, gradually fading away.

"How do I choose, Lady?" he asked. He very much feared he would make a mistake.

"Use your eyes and listen to your gut. Feel." she answered.

Thomas's gaze roamed along the walls, thinking about all of the lives that these weapons had taken over the years, the centuries. He pressed his own lips together in a thin line. As he waited, he began to quiver inside as the weight of time and agony and death wove their menace into his awareness.

He shook his head, trying to dispel his disquiet. He centered himself again and stood quietly.

Slowly, slowly, he recognized a pull toward the left side of the room. He moved toward the attraction with hesitant steps. He raised his arm and allowed his fingers to lightly touch each of the weapons as he moved carefully along the wall. Sword after sword passed under his fingertips.

He'd almost reached the end of the room when he felt heat on his fingers. His mouth went dry and his stomach clenched with excitement and dread. His hand moved without his thinking to grasp the hilt of a sword at least eight hand spans long - longer and heavier than any he had ever used. The blade rested on a rack above its scabbard.

Carefully he lifted it from its place among these weapons of war.

A graceful extension of the guard curved from the left quillon to a Dragon's eye stone mounted in the Dragon claw pommel. The grip was wrapped in finest deep brown deer hide. Steel gleamed in magelight. For a moment he thought he saw runes light along the fuller in that gleam. A shiver ran up his arm. Certainty filled his mind and heart. *This is mine!* He grinned fiercely and thrust the sword to full extension. Its balance was perfect. Recovering, he turned toward Lady Aeden, the sword raised in front of his face in salute.

A deep thrumming sound filled the room. *What is that?* He grasped the sword tighter as he looked wildly at the windows and then the corners, trying to locate the source. It emanated from the stones themselves. His body vibrated with its resonance.

Lady Aeden hummed deep in her throat, echoing the sound that filled the room. Magelight flashed a deeper blue from her eyes. "That is a powerful choice, my lord." She smiled and nodded congratulations. He shook his head, trying to clear his mind. The noise was almost frightening in its intensity.

What is that sound? Why is it happening now? Is this sword something special? Thomas glanced again at the blade and saw the runes glimmering along its length.

He felt as if a missing piece of him-self had returned. He knew he was complete as he looked back at Aeden, grinned and nodded to her. He took the scabbard down from its rack and sheathed the sword. He removed his belt and threaded the scabbard onto it. As he belted it on, the volume of the thrumming increased. He shook his head again as he and Lady Aeden moved to the doors of the armory.

The thrumming faded slowly away as Thomas, with his new sword, walked out the door.

Chapter 9

Mannan's head jerked up in disbelief. The spell book he was reading fell from numb hands to the table with a thud. The fields of magic that bound him to this place flared with power. Power that he'd not felt for a very, very long time.

The High Draiolc, the Dark's own sorcerer, stood in shock and consternation. His anger began to grow. As it did, his face and body transformed from one visage and physique to another. For a moment, he was thin and old, with wispy hair and wrinkled face. Next, he was a handsome, robust young man. He shifted through four seemings as he struggled for mental balance.

He turned from the table and strode to the three-legged wooden stand that dominated the north side of his workspace. He whipped the silk covering off of a giant crystal ball the size of a dinner plate. The covering drifted to the floor as he settled his fingertips on either side of the crystal. He closed his eyes and waited for his will to activate the energy within it.

Slowly the crystal warmed. He opened his eyes and stared into the crystal. He pictured his minion whom he had corrupted in the town outside of Red Dragon's Keep. With a snap of his mind like a whip, he sent his thoughts toward the man. He felt the connection grab and the man recoil in fear. He surrounded the man's thoughts and took over his body. He looked out at the dimly lit tavern filled with villagers taking their mid-meal.

Rising abruptly, he hurried the man's body out of the tavern and turned toward the Tower. Villagers called greetings as he passed and he waved at them, but didn't stop. He made his way through the Dragon Tower wall gate, turned left and continued into the stables. He grabbed the nearest stable-boy and shook him roughly.

"Have you seen or heard anything strange from the Tower? I was told in the village there were mysterious things happening here."

"No. There was an odd noise a little while ago, but it went away. Let me go!" The stable-boy struggled to jerk his shirt out of the man's hands. The man reached out and smacked his hand hard against the stable-boy's ear. He gave him another good shake, and shoved him away.

"Get back to work," he ordered.

The man strode out of the stable, and stopped, facing the Tower. He put his hands on his hips and slowly scanned the area in front of him. Dragon Tower, kitchen garden, weapons practice area. His eyes were drawn to the armory. He knew what was held there.

Abruptly, Mannan withdrew from the man's mind, taking all knowledge of his sorcery with him.

A Sword of Light had awakened.

Mannan stood frozen in thought before the crystal.

No matter. The ambush set for the Duke will seal his fate. There is nothing they can do about it. The Sword of Light is only one, not many. Who holds it does not matter. The plan proceeds.

He removed his hands from the crystal. He bent down and retrieved the silk covering and placed it gently over the orb.

He walked back to the table, picked up the spell-book and returned to reading.

Chapter 10

The Duke's cavalcade stopped for the night four days past the Lake of Wings, the largest lake between Red Dragon's Keep and Cathair Ri. The Samphir River, much broader here because of tributary flows, surged against its banks, making it unsafe to approach except in sheltered coves carved out by running water. They were almost to Great Falls and the river crossing he planned to make there. Another five or six days would see them at Cathair Ri.

"My Lord, the flour has spoiled and two of the water barrels are dry," reported a lieutenant who had walked up behind him.

Lord Tom Arach finished running the dandy brush over his horse's coat. He turned toward the lieutenant shifting nervously from foot to foot. He rested his hand casually on the horse's back.

"How do you know?" he asked.

"The cook told me. I've brought it to you," the lieutenant responded.

"Let's go talk to the cook," the Duke said, with a final pat on his horse's rump. He tossed the brush into the equipment bucket as they passed the end of the picket line.

They made their way through the camp past the tents that the soldiers were setting up in ordered rows. The smoke from the cook fire rose lazily into the still air. Once out of the mountains that sheltered Red Dragon's Keep, late summer still held the land in its grasp. Ripening grasses rippled in the breezes that wandered the valley. The trees along the river were starting their yearly change to red and orange and gold, signaling the coming of fall.

"Tell me," Lord Tom said, as he and the lieutenant reached the supply wagon where the cook stood waiting.

"Lord, I don't know how this happened. Well, yes I do. Mold was obviously put in with the flour when the barrels were filled. There are small holes drilled through the bottoms of the water barrels. Just big enough to allow small dribbles to escape, nothing that would be noticed," the cook responded. "I have no idea who did it," he said with a grimace, his eyes narrow, lips thin.

"How much flour do we have left? Have you checked the other supplies?" Lord Tom asked, and then sighed.

"Lieutenant, please go and ask Ladies Jenni and Anne, and Lord Jeremy to meet me here." He shook his head in frustration. "I knew things were going too well."

He turned back to the cook. "Get some men and check all the rest of the supplies. There's a village a day ahead where we might be able to replace what we've lost."

"Yes, my Lord. I'll get right on it." The cook walked back to the cook fire, gave the kettle filled with stew a quick stir and bellowed at his men to report to him.

Lady Jenni walked toward him from the middle of the camp. As she reached him, she turned her head to watch the cook ordering his men to the supply wagons. "What's happened?" she asked, her brows lowering over her eyes.

"Sabotage," he answered tersely. "It's felt too easy. I've been waiting for something to happen."

"I know what you mean," Lady Jenni answered with her own sigh. "What's the damage?"

"Spoiled flour and leaking water barrels. I suspect all of them have been drilled," he answered. "The men are checking everything else. I won't be surprised if there's more."

Lady Anne and Lord Jeremy, parents to Cameron and Evan, walked toward them, followed the lieutenant from the opposite side of the camp.

They'd joined the Duke's caravan at the confluence of the Caladen and Banuisk rivers. The sisters nodded to each other.

"Someone, or maybe more than one someone, has sabotaged our supplies. You might want to check yours to see if anything is amiss," Lord Tom told them. "We've got moldy flour and leaking water barrels. The water barrels should be easy enough to repair and fill, and we might be able to replace the flour at the next village."

Something just doesn't feel right. We'd better put everyone on alert."

"I've been having this niggling feeling that someone is watching us," Lady Anne told the three. Tall and slender, her dark brown hair pulled back in a tail that trailed down the back of her linen blouse, she looked at her sister with worry in her chocolate brown eyes. "What about you, Jenni? Anything?"

The sisters were known for their ability to sense things.

Lady Jenni shrugged. "Just a little itch, like someone is trying to read me," she responded.

"Well, we'll do the best we can." Jeremy spoke thoughtfully, his hands on his hips. "You're right, Tom. We'll alert our men, too." As tall as Lord Tom, he towered over the two women, his wiry strength evident in his controlled movements. "Do you think there's a traitor here now?" He rubbed a hand in distraction over his very short brown hair. "Any way to find out?" he asked, scanning the campsite with his deeply set blue eyes. His long face was twisted in a grimace of concern.

"I think the only thing we can do is put a watch on the wagons. I'd lay odds that this happened back at the Tower, though," Lord Tom responded. "Ladies, if either of you notice anything..."

"We'll make sure you're the first to know," they chorused in unison.

Lord Tom grimaced. "I'm sure you will."

Lord Jeremy laughed and clapped him on the shoulder. "Anne, let's get the watch set. It's almost time for dinner." The four scattered to prepare as best they could for whatever might come.

Chapter 11

"Eagan, you stand watch so we don't get caught," Calen ordered.

Eagan darted his small squinty eyes furtively at the other squires and then along the walls, making sure that no one else was near enough to hear them. His hands nervously plucked at his dirty shirt and then at the growing hole in the seam of his trousers. Horse's heads hung out of some of the stall windows to the left and right as they drowsed in the increasingly rare afternoon warmth.

Calen, Eagan, Newlan and Tristan huddled behind the stables after mid-meal. Everyone shifted shoulders and feet uneasily. If they didn't hurry they would be late for their afternoon chores and lessons. They'd earn punishment if they were tardy.

"Ever since Garan was exiled, I've wanted to take out Thomas," Calen spoke softly and viciously. "It's all his fault that we can't bully the other squires and skullies anymore.

I've tried to hurt that brat every time we spar and nothing seems to get through. Oh, he gets bruises alright, but that's all. Have any of you had any better luck?" Calen cursed savagely under his breath. His dark brown eyes shone with anger. His black hair, black shirt and trousers made him look older and more sinister than the others.

A chorus of 'No's' answered Calen's question. He shook his head, lips tight, arms rigid at his sides, hands clenched into fists. He pounded one fist against his leg. "We have *got* to *do* something. We're on a deadline here. Does anyone have any ideas at all?"

Tristan cleared his throat nervously. He was tall and thin and looked like he hadn't bathed in a week. "Why don't we just ambush him in the Tower and stick a knife in him? That should be easy enough."

"Right," said Newlan sarcastically. He slouched against the stable wall, arms crossed over his chest. "Just lure him into a dark corridor and kill him. Right. Do you know what would happen then? The Tower gets closed down tight and every single person in it is tortured until they find the killer. Good idea." He snorted.

"Well, do you have a better idea?" asked Calen sharply.

"I've been thinking we could sabotage the training course. Maybe set up a deadfall on the running path. We could grease the balance log or fray the climb rope." Newlan shrugged his shoulders.

Calen looked at him speculatively. "Do you think we can do that?"

"If all of you help, sure."

"Shhhh!" Eagan urgently gestured for all of them to be quiet. Voices echoed through the windows of the stable. Two guards patrolled the aisle between the horse stalls. They were comparing the use of a staff against a halberd.

After the guards had passed, Calen bent forward and motioned all of them closer. "Let's do this tomorrow, early. Each of us will take an obstacle and make sure it will fail. Thomas always goes first on the course, so one of them should get him. Eagan, you take the low jump. Newlan, the log walk. Tristan, the rope climb. I'll take the roll-over log." Each nodded sharply as Calen assigned them their targets.

Calen smiled grimly and waved at the others to leave. He stood there, frowning in thought for a short time, imagining what would happen when their sabotage killed Thomas. He grinned wickedly as he walked out from behind the stables toward his next class.

Chapter 12

Granda stumbled and almost fell. Marta reached out and grabbed his arm to steady him. "Thank you, Marta. I'm sorry I'm so slow. Happens when you get old." He shook his head in frustration. "Could you ask your da if we could stop for a rest? I'm awful tired."

Marta leaned over and kissed him on his sweaty cheek. "Of course I'll ask. Here. Let's get you settled on the grass." She helped him wobble over to the side of the road where lush green grass had once stood. Now it was dead and dried. Fall was steadily advancing. Granda slowly lowered himself to the ground and gave a loud sigh. Marta swung the water-skin off of her shoulder and gave it to him. "I'll be right back."

The column of holders and their families continued to trudge past her on the track that led to Red Dragon's Keep. They had left the Steading the day after the Demon attack. For five days they had been walking toward what they hoped was safety. She felt like she had been walking forever.

Sheep, goats, cattle and horses the Steading and holders owned raised a cloud of dust from the track. Babies cried, mothers soothed and children, now too tired to play, tramped morosely next to their parents. Wagons creaked and ungreased wheels squealed as they passed by, carrying as much food, fodder and possessions as they would hold.

Marta trotted along the side of the track on the dead grass. She exchanged hellos with those she hurried past. Her mother put her in charge of helping her granda when they left the Steading and she had been caring for him the entire way. The refugees could only move as fast as he and the other elderlies could.

Faolan, Marta's father, strode along the track, his face set and stern. His long strides covered the ground, seemingly without effort. Marta slowed only a little as she reached his side, matching his pace. "Da, Granda needs to rest. Can we take a break?"

Faolan looked at her with blank eyes for a few strides. His attention snapped to her and his light brown eyes looked at her instead of whatever he'd been thinking about. He looked around as he walked, then checked the sky for the time of day. They'd been traveling for several candlemarks and the afternoon was well spent.

"Yes, it's time to find a defensible place to set up for the night. Run back along the line and tell everyone it's time to rest. Send your brothers up here. We'll scout for a place to camp."

He walked over to the side of the track, pulling off the floppy straw hat that sheltered his head from the sun. Sweat ran down the side of his face. He unslung his water-skin from his shoulder as he reached the edge and folded himself down to the ground wearily. He untied the top of the skin and took a large swallow of lukewarm water.

The families walking behind him followed his lead and moved to the verge of the road.

"Ok," Marta croaked on a dry throat. Her father handed her the water-skin without a word. She took a sip, handed it back and turned to run back down the line. "You're doing a good job, Marta. Thank you."

"Thanks, Da." She swung into a slow trot and shouted to those she passed to take a break. A third of the way down the column, she stopped as she reached her brothers. Both of them carried heavy packs on their backs and someone's toddler on a hip. Voices rose in query and conversation as everyone welcomed the pause in relentless travel.

"Jaiman, Kevin. Da wants you up front to scout for a camp-site for tonight."

Both young men sighed, and then passed the toddlers to their mothers walking beside them. "Ok. We're on our way," Jaiman, her older brother responded. They threw their packs into the wagon that they were trailing behind.

Marta continued on, letting everyone know that they were stopping for the night, until she reached the end of the line of footsore holders. The last oldsters were just passing her granda. The holders gratefully moved off of the track and settled on its verge.

"Come on Granda. Let's get you up closer to the others. She walked with him as he shuffled after his friends, and finally caught up with them.

Jaiman and Kevin jogged along the line that snaked up the track. It was rising steadily as it approached the first pass through the Dragon's Spine. The little band of refugees had two more to navigate before they reached Red Dragon's Keep.

"Jaiman, do you think we can get everyone there safely?" panted Kevin as they hurried.

"It won't be for lack of trying," answered Jaiman. "All of the men here, and most of the women, have weapons. I have a feeling we're going to need them before we get there."

Faolan stood as the young men arrived, retying the neck of his water skin and slinging its strap over his shoulder. His short, graying dark brown hair was plastered to his head with sweat.

"We need to scout out half a mile. Look for a stream and an opening in the forest large enough to handle all of us. I think I recall one right around this spot. Meet back here in a quarter of a candlemark." He slapped each of them on their shoulder. "Go."

Each young man took a side of the track and stepped into the forest to look for a clearing.

Faolan looked at the long line of his holders stretching back toward the Steading. He waved at the two closest men. "Let's get everyone bunched up on the track. There's a clearing somewhere close and I want everyone ready to move and set up camp."

The two men nodded at him and set off along the sides of the column, chivying their friends and neighbors to close up ranks and join those near the front of the column.

$ $ $

The sun slowly dropped closer to the horizon. Marta looked uneasily at the line of trees that bordered the track. She felt awfully exposed here. A shiver of fear raised the hairs on the back of her neck.

Shouts traveled down the length of the column of holders. A camp-site had been found about a hundred yards into the forest on the west side of the road. The line began to move.

The holders wound their way between the trees into a small meadow, startling a herd of deer from their grazing. A narrow stream bordered the meadow. Children ran toward the water for welcome relief from dry throats.

Everyone gratefully dropped packs to the ground where they intended to rest and others guided their horse-drawn and hand pushed carts into a line that would provide some shelter from an attack from the road. The horses were hobbled and left to graze on the dried grass, younger boys put in charge of watching them.

Fires were started and food was prepared. Marta scooped a bowl of stew from the pot and took it to her granda. She found him leaning against a tree, fast asleep. She shook his shoulder gently. "Wake up, Granda. I've brought you supper."

With a jerk and a snort, her granda woke. He grinned at her, face drawn in tired lines. "Just taking a little nap," he said.

"I know," she said kindly. "Best to eat first and then sleep," she recommended.

"You go get yours, girl. I'll be fine."

"Yes, sir," she said, smiling at him. She hoped desperately that he was strong enough to make it to Red Dragon's Keep.

Chapter 13

Thomas speared a carrot and chunk of potato from his bread trencher with his knife and took a bite, chewing quickly. The vegetables filled him up yet still left room for the golden roasted chicken on his plate.

Tapestries depicting epic battles from wars long past covered the walls of the main hall of the Dragon Tower. A great mural was painted on the stones above the huge fireplace that warmed the room. Worked in brilliant colors, the scene depicted the final days of the first Great War between Dragons, their human allies and Demon hordes. Glass jewels had been set into the mortar between stones, glittering in the reflected light of candles. When not used for meals, the Duke met with his councilors and held court for emissaries and peers in this room. The head table was placed in front of the fireplace where logs were kept burning throughout the fall and winter. It faced the ranks of tables that were filled with residents of the Keep.

Simon, the chamberlain, entered the hall from the left and walked briskly to the table where Thomas, Owen and Breanna were seated.

"My Lord, a rider at the gate begs to speak with you. He has been sent ahead of your cousins Lord Cameron and Lord Evan who are riding here for safety."

Thomas paused with food half way to his mouth, and then carefully placed his knife back on his plate. His cheeks flushed. He wasn't used to 'My Lord'. That was his father.

"Please have the rider brought in," he told Simon with a nod.

"Yes, my Lord."

Owen and Breanna snickered. Thomas shot them a glare.

Gregory strode into the room, his face a study in concern, as the chamberlain escorted the rider to the head table.

"What is your name, rider?" asked Thomas. He'd heard his father say the same thing countless times.

"Colin, my Lord" the rider answered. He bowed. He was covered with dust and mud and blood from his ride to the Keep. "Lord and Lady Gobhlan have sent their sons Cameron and Evan to you from Falcon's Spire for safety. The Lord and Lady have been called to the capital and there is unrest in the countryside."

Thomas frowned and glanced at Gregory. Gregory shook his head as he looked at him. "My Lord, I'll have Simon ready two rooms for your cousins." A crooked smile crossed his face. "Lad, this is happening more quickly than your father and I thought possible. We must talk as soon as the boys are settled."

Thomas slowly nodded his head. He swallowed hard.

What is going on? Am I finally going to be included in Gregory's and Captain Mathin's planning? Maybe I can really help.

A little shiver of fear and excitement ran down his spine.

Dinner was cleared away and Thomas was helping to stack the tables and benches against the wall when the convoy from Falcon's Spire finally arrived.

Gregory stopped him. "My Lord, please allow the skullies to clear the room. We have much to discuss. Let's get your cousins settled, and then meet in my office."

Thomas slowly put the chairs he'd picked up back under the table. *This change feels really strange. I've always helped with the cleanup before.*

He turned and looked at the older man. Gregory was tall and thin, dressed in brown leather trousers and jerkin over a red tunic. A frown carved deep furrows between his brown eyes and his lips pressed together in a thin line. His white hair was parted neatly and trimmed above his ears on the sides. It fell to his collar in back. Gregory had been with Lord Tom since the two had joined the King's army to fight in the last war.

Two boys hurried through the doors from the forecourt into the great hall, escorted by the sergeant of their guard.

Cameron, the same age as Breanna, and Evan, the youngest of all of the children, looked tired and unhappy. The sergeant saluted Thomas and Gregory, right fist to chest.

"My Lord, I've brought them safe. We were attacked about twenty miles north of the Keep. I'm the senior man left. Our captain and lieutenant were killed and five wounded. Do you have a midach or a crionna baen, a wise-woman?"

Thomas's eyes widened in dismay. Owen and Breanna gasped in unison.

Gregory answered, "Lord Thomas, I'll send for Moirra. She's one of the town crionna baen, the wise-women."

Thomas nodded his head.

"Your name?" Gregory asked as he turned to the man.

"Sergeant Linden, sir," the soldier answered.

"Follow the skullies to the infirmary, Sergeant. Settle the wounded there. The rest of your guard can find bunks in the barracks. See the staff sergeant for that. I believe they are still at dinner."

The sergeant saluted. "Yes sir," he said and turned to follow the skullies.

Soldiers carried trunks into the room. Gregory motioned for a skully to lead them to the chambers set aside for Cameron and Evan.

"Boys, do you want to eat or would you like to bathe before bed?" asked Gregory.

Cameron, as thin as a rail, looked at him with fear and sorrow in his brilliant amber eyes. His dark blond hair was matted with mud from the road.

"Please, could we eat? We couldn't stop because of the attack," he choked out. Evan clutched Cameron's right arm. He and Evan looked badly frightened by the Demons that had attacked them. Evan, a solid boy, nodded vigorously, his white blond hair as dirty as his brothers. His blue eyes glistened with unshed tears.

"Of course. You know where the kitchen is. Tell Jalyn to set out the chicken and vegetables and fruit we had for dinner," Gregory said. Cameron and Evan headed for the kitchen, shepherded by Simon.

"Come to my office, Thomas. It's best to discuss what's happening where others can't hear." They walked in silence from the great hall and down the corridor to Gregory's domain. Thomas's eyes were drawn guiltily to the wall where he had listened to the scouts report as he walked into the office.

Thomas sat in the chair across the desk from the seneschal. The desk was covered with neat stacks of paper waiting for Gregory's attention. Gregory took out his pipe and slowly filled it, then set a match to light it. Fragrant smoke curled lazily to the ceiling and spread along the dark wooden beams there.

"Your father and mother, as well as your Uncle Jeremy and Aunt Anne, were called to the capital because the Ciardha - the Dark - and its minion Demons, have risen in the south and west. The Reaches have been breached in too many places to name. Fasach is fighting for its very existence and Fearmhar has been attacked. I am very concerned with the attacks on your cousin's caravan. We must hurry with setting defenses in place. Have you talked to Captain Mathin about them?"

"Yes," Thomas responded. "We've been discussing how to feed and shelter all of the Steaders, holders, freemen, and their families coming to Red Dragon's Keep."

"It's not just that, Lord Thomas. We need a strategy to kill the Demons. I've read through every record I've had time for and can't find anything that explains what these monsters are doing or why, what works to drive them away or to kill them. We need to send out scouts and try to find some pattern. We need someone to read more of the old records to see if anything can be found to help us. You, Owen and Breanna, and possibly Cameron and Evan, can help with that. I'll have the records moved to the Solar, if that's agreeable?"

"Of course," Thomas said faintly.

Chapter 14

In the early morning light, Thomas jogged along the path that ran beside the Keep. It was cold, and his breath puffed out in a cloud of white with each stride. The ground was hard but still free from snow. He continued through the village and into the forests on the slope of the mountain to the north. He and the other squires and guards trained on the path every day. Half way along the mountain path, a series of obstacles had been constructed to make the most of their conditioning runs.

Thomas bounced over the first low jump made of a log resting on stumps on either side of the path. The ground on the far side of the jump was wet and spongy, but he saw it and jumped far enough that he missed the wet patch.

Panting with exertion, he continued along the path. He jogged around a tree as the path turned to the right. A chest high "roll-over log" set on high stumps cut from trees on either side of the path blocked his way.

He slapped it with his right hand and lifted up to land on it with his chest. Pain flared through his body as his hand, clothing and chest were torn by jagged pieces of sharpened metal hammered into the wood.

He gasped in agony and pushed off of the log. Blood flowed down his chest and from his hand as he landed on his knees and rolled to his back. His left hand grabbed his right as he cradled it against his bleeding chest. The men-at-arms following him on the course put on a burst of speed when they saw him fall to the ground. They pulled their belt knives as they approached and formed a ring around the fallen heir, scanning for any threat.

The corporal leading the guard detail knelt at his side. "My Lord, are you all right? What happened?"

Thomas groaned and raised his hands away from his chest. He was dizzy and felt sick to his stomach. He reluctantly looked at his right hand, not wanting to see the damage.

He stared in amazement. As he watched, the blood flowing from his badly lacerated palm slowed, then stopped, and the cuts began to close. The pain in his chest started to ebb. He lifted his cloak and shirt to see the same thing happening.

The corporal's face blanched. The only evidence that remained was his shredded bloody shirt.

Maybe the magic I've been practicing is helping my body to heal. I need to talk to Lady Aeden.

He rolled to his stomach and pushed himself to his feet. "I'm fine. Somebody sabotaged the roll-over log. Check and see if the other obstacles have been damaged."

The men scattered along the training course as Thomas went back to look at the roll-over log. He counted thirty of what looked like the broken tips of swords sticking out of the wood. He slowly moved his hand about five inches above the log, searching for any magical trace of who might have done this. He knew he wasn't an expert, but he thought he might be able to sense something. He shook his head in frustration. Nothing.

One of the men shouted that the log walk had been undercut enough to collapse if stepped on. Another reported that the climb rope had been frayed at the very top. If Thomas had climbed it, he could have fallen and broken both legs.

Shaken, Thomas ordered the men back to the Keep. It was very clear that someone wanted him dead.

§ § §

Thomas rounded the corner from the stables to the practice field at an easy jog. He headed toward the salle where Lady Aeden was teaching unarmed combat to the squires.

She ought to be just about done, he thought. *I've got to tell her what happened this morning.*

He pushed the door open and entered just as Aeden threw Eagan over her shoulder to land with a solid thud on his back in the sand at the center of the room. The boards that normally covered the sandpit were stacked next to the benches on the north side of the room.

Aeden's hair was bound back into a tight braid that was held in a roll at the base of her neck. Her linen shirt and trousers were fitted tightly to keep anyone from grabbing loose fabric.

The other squires snickered and laughed out loud as Eagan groaned in humiliation.

"Serves you right," Newlan gloated. "You shouldn't have tripped me."

"Enough for today," ordered Aeden. "Rake the sand, put the floor boards back and then off to your lessons." The boys scurried to their tasks.

"How may I help you, Lord Thomas?" she asked with a small bow.

"Lady Aeden. I need to talk to you in private. Where would you suggest?"

Aeden gave him a sharp look and raised one eyebrow. She glanced at the squires. "Help me return this gear to the equipment room."

Thomas helped her gather up the training knives, quarterstaffs and batons that she used for her classes. They carried the gear down the hall past the weapons room to the equipment storage room on the opposite side of the corridor. Shelves held heavy gloves, padded jackets, and helmets. He put his armful of knives and batons on their racks as Aeden did the same with the quarterstaffs.

"Lady, I don't know if you've heard, but something happened this morning on my training run. Someone tampered with everything on the obstacle course. I cut my hands and chest on the roll-over log. That part is important, but what scared me the most was the healing that followed. Nothing like that has ever happened before. Could it have happened because I've been practicing magic?"

Both of Aeden's eyebrows rose and her eyes widened. "Show me," she exclaimed as she reached for his hand.

Thomas lifted his hand and placed it, palm-up, in hers. She bent to look very closely at his palm. No scars were visible.

"Anywhere else?" she asked.

"My chest," he answered.

She motioned for him to lift his shirt. No marks remained. She stared at his chest.

"The only creatures I know who can heal like this are Dragons, and I only know that because it was written down in the records from long ago. There must be some other explanation. Do you know of any magical healers in your ancestors?"

Thomas shook his head, more than a little afraid of her intensity.

"After I was hurt, I stayed on the ground. I felt sick and dizzy. Do you have any idea why that happened?"

Aeden looked at him. "It's odd. Heavy use of magic causes those symptoms. It means that your body used its own resources to heal itself." She shook her head. "Magic usually doesn't happen unless the mage calls for it. We need to study this closely."

"I thought maybe you could see if any traces of whoever might have done this were left on the obstacle course," he said.

"Good thought. Let's go now and check."

Thomas followed Aeden from the salle. They made their way along the path to the first obstacle. At the sight of spongy ground on the far side of the first jump, Aeden shook her head. "No way to tell anything from this. Anyone could have dumped water here."

At the roll-over log, Aeden stood for a long time, arms extended, and palms down, sensing who might have touched the log or the sharpened pieces of metal. After several minutes, she lowered her arms and turned to Thomas. Her face was grim.

"It is Calen, Tristan, Eagan and Newlan," she said heavily. She shrugged her shoulders and shook her head. "We might as well go back to the Keep and let Gregory know. This needs to be taken care of, now."

$$\$ \, \$ \, \$$

"Bring the prisoners to the great hall," Thomas ordered the two guards stationed on either side of the door into the great hall. Captain Mathin stood next to him, his fingers white knuckled as he strangled his heavy belt, legs spread. Teeth clenched, lips flat, brows lowered, he looked like he wanted to kill something.

"What am I supposed to do with them?" Thomas asked. "They are noblemen's sons! I want them punished, but I don't think I can just send them home like Garan."

The captain pursed his lips, let go of his belt and crossed his arms over his chest.

"Lad, you're right. They are indeed noble born, so best to send them to the King. I think you should let him judge them."

Thomas gave a sharp nod. "Good idea. Thank you."

Two guards jerked the four squires into the great hall. The weight of the manacles binding their wrists pulled their hands down below their waists. The clash of their ankle chains filled the room as they were forced to move their legs in unison.

The guards shoved them into a ragged line in front of Thomas. He sat in his father's chair, his sword resting across his lap.

"Lady Aeden discovered your treachery. You failed in your attempt to harm me or anyone else, if that was your goal. Do you have anything to say for yourselves?"

The young men stood silent, still defiant in their captivity. They hadn't counted on Lady Aeden and her magic.

Thomas shook his head in disgust. "You were well treated here. Your betrayal is beneath contempt. I wish I could have your punishment, but wiser thinking has prevailed." He nodded at Captain Mathin with respect.

"You will be taken in chains and under guard to Cathair Ri. The King will judge you and decide your punishment."

All four faces went white. Eyes wide, they looked at each other. No one said a word.

Calen looked at Thomas with narrowed glittering eyes, a snarl twisting his mouth. His hatred was evident, but he said nothing.

"Take them away," Thomas ordered the guards.

Chapter 15

October was two days away and cold, ice, and snow should have blanketed the country. Instead, the weather held frigid but dry. Against all tradition, the Ciardha sent raiders who had been turned from vassals to monsters ripping at the outlaying farms, burning homes and killing stock and freeholders.

Lady Aeden pushed Thomas relentlessly, demanding that he learn how to use every weapon in the armory as well as unarmed combat. Coupled with that training, half of his time was spent with Gregory, learning about contracts, negotiations, and Keep management.

What little time remained, he, his brother, sister, and cousins spent reading old records, looking for answers to desperate questions. He often felt like a top, spinning out of control. Every night he fell into bed exhausted.

Thomas walked into his room following a full day of weapons training, lessons and practicing statesmanship. He unbuckled his sword belt as he walked to its rack, hung it up, turned and fell onto his bed, arms spread wide.

I hurt. I can't do this anymore. Why did I ever want to learn to fight? He whimpered. Every muscle in his body seemed to throb in time with his heart. *I wish my healing power, whatever it is, would stop these aches. Ha.*

He was sweaty and covered in dirt. He flipped to his side and groaned. *I've got to get ready for dinner. Bath first.* He rolled over and pushed himself up from the bed.

He looked at himself in the mirror that hung on the wall next to the wardrobe. The sleeves of his shirt were getting shorter by the day, and his wrists stuck out by at least two inches. His trousers seemed to be shrinking too. He'd soon have to ask for larger clothes. He had grown taller. His arms and legs had muscles that he hadn't seen before.

He pulled off his trousers, shirt and tunic, tossing each piece over the waiting chair. His chamberlain would take them to be cleaned. He shrugged into his robe, grabbed a towel and headed for the bathing room.

Owen pulled open the door of his room and rushed out as Thomas strode past. He was as filthy as his brother. "Thomas, Lady Aeden said that we could spar together tomorrow." His voice tended to squeak up when he was excited. Thomas grinned. Owen had grown taller, too, over the past weeks.

"Good! I've been watching while you practiced. You're learning to whack the training dummy almost every time."

"I really like doing that. Aeden says that I'm good with knife fighting too."

They reached the door to the bathing chamber, and Thomas pushed it open.

Cameron and Evan were both there, ready to take their own baths. They had been set as pages to Thomas and Owen, so they wore the same dust, dirt, and contusions as their cousins. They were learning how to clean armor and take care of the horses that the fighting men used. It was hard dirty work, and they loved it. They'd been considered too young to do any of it at Falcon's Spire.

The room was pleasantly humid after the chill of the hallway as a large fire burned in the fireplace across from the door. Four beaten-copper tubs were filled with hot water heated in a huge cauldron suspended over the fire. The boiling water helped keep the room warm.

Thomas dropped his towel on the bench along the left wall and stepped into the tub nearest him. He breathed a sigh as he lowered himself into the hot water. Muscles began to loosen. Cameron, dark blond and thin as a rail, laughed as Owen ducked completely under the water. Evan, bright blond and sturdy, washed quickly.

"What's your hurry, Evan?" Thomas asked.

"I'm going to the kitchen for a snack before dinner," Evan answered. "I'm hungry."

"You're always hungry," Thomas exclaimed.

"Thomas, have you heard anything from Mother or Father?" asked Evan.

"I'm sorry Evan. I haven't heard anything about them," answered Thomas. "We just need to keep training and get ready to help."

Dejected and clearly missing them, Evan bowed his head and went back to washing.

Owen jumped out of his tub and went to the cauldron for more hot water.

"Owen, can you get me some?" Thomas asked.

"Sure!" Owen laughed. He grabbed a bucket, filled it, walked over and poured some into each tub, deliberately hitting bare chests. Squeals of outrage echoed through the room.

Thomas leaned back and just relaxed.

"I've heard the soldiers talking about Demons. They said they are really hard to kill, and that they run right up swords and spears," Cameron informed them.

"I heard in the village that there are ghosts in the undercroft. Skullies are afraid to go down there," Owen added, trying to take control of the conversation.

The dinner bell tolled through the Tower. Water sloshed over the sides of the tubs as all of the boys stood up and stepped out. The overflow drained toward an opening cut in the floor and was carried away by piping on the side of the Dragon Tower.

Cameron snapped his wet towel at Owen. Owen howled and jumped on Cameron. Laughing, they rolled across the wet stone floor.

"Hurry up, you guys," Thomas shouted. He finished drying, wrapped the towel around his hips, swung his robe around his shoulders and pulled the door open. He sprinted down the hall to his room. The floors were cold!

Once in his room, he jerked on the trousers laid out on his bed, pulled on house-shoes and shrugged into his shirt and tunic. Simon had already come and gone.

Thomas headed out of his room, pulling the heavy door closed behind him. Night came early this time of year, as did the chill in the hall. Best to keep the warmth inside the room.

Magelight flickered in globes set into iron brackets on the wall. No one knew how the lights were made, what kept them burning all the time. No smoke rose to the ceiling to fill the Tower with throat-choking stench. Magelight glowed all the time, making the Tower corridors easy to use. No shadows hid people or ghosts.

Thomas took the narrow stairs that curved to his left two at a time down to the main hall. Savory smells of roasting pork and potatoes made his mouth water. Reaching the bottom, he stopped and pulled his shirt and tunic straight, trying to make the sleeves longer. He shook his head and walked to the head table.

Breanna and Owen hurried down the stairs after him. Owen sat on Thomas's right, Breanna next to Owen. Cameron and Evan skidded into the hall, and then walked sedately to the table. They took their seats on the other side of the two center chairs reserved for the Lord and Lady.

Skullies brought trays of food to the table under the watchful eye of Gregory.

Thomas stabbed a piece of sliced mutton with his belt knife and folded it into his mouth. Juices from the meat dribbled down his chin. He used a finger to wipe them up and into his mouth. His wooden goblet of water was soon emptied. The others made quick work of the meal.

"Gregory, Captain Mathin. I'd like to talk to you both after dinner, if you don't mind," Thomas said, wiping his chin. Gregory gave him a sharp look.

"Of course, my Lord, as soon as dessert is done. Jalyn has peach pudding for us tonight," Gregory replied.

Chapter 16

Skullies worked to clear the dishes from the tables following the meal as the others arranged themselves in front of the fire, playing table games and reading lessons.

Thomas followed Gregory and Captain Mathin through the arch on the right-hand wall and turned left down the hall to Gregory's office.

Gregory pushed the door open and waved toward the brown damask wingback chairs placed in front of his desk. Mathin and Thomas sat.

"How may I serve you, my Lord?" Gregory pulled a pipe from his belt and filled it with tobacco from the leather pouch belted at his waist as he spoke. Tamping the tobacco into the bowl with his thumb, he walked to the fireplace where a fire burned to warm the room. He bent and touched a taper to the fire, then lifted it to the bowl of his pipe.

He drew air through the stem of the pipe, shook the flame from the taper and tossed it into the fire, turned and walked to the chair behind the desk. Smoke curled toward the ceiling. He brushed ash from the front of his gray-brown tunic and sat down.

"We've caught traitors living here and ended that threat," Thomas said. "Captain Mathin stopped me this morning after quarterstaff practice and told me that he has received reports of raiders or Demons getting closer to the Keep." Thomas nodded at Captain Mathin. "What more needs to be done?" he asked.

Captain Mathin nodded gravely. He'd changed into a soft, old blue shirt and buckskin trousers before dinner.

"I know both of you are in charge, but I'd like to know what you've planned," said Thomas.

Gregory set his pipe on its stand, leaned back in his chair and steepled his hands in front of him, resting his forefingers on his lips. He gazed unseeing at the far wall.

Captain Mathin chuckled. "I told you it wouldn't be long. He's absorbing everything I can teach him as fast as I tell it to him. He's even had some very good ideas about rotating the watch and filling the cistern."

Thomas's face flushed with embarrassment. He looked at Captain Mathin.

"Oh no, my Lord, no complaints," the captain said, shaking his head and raising his hands. "You're getting to be as sharp as that sword Lady Aeden is starting to let you use."

Gregory slapped his hands down on the arms of his chair and murmured, "So be it." He pushed himself out of the chair and moved to the left wall.

A large map of Ard An Tir, the continent that held the four countries of Ard Ri, Talamh, Fasach and Fearmhar, hung from the ceiling beam at the top of the wall. The map was filled with glass headed pins of various colors.

Each color represented an attack and when it occurred. He pointed to Fasach, the desert lands that lay south of Ard Ri.

"We know that the Ciardha Demons have been moving north from Fasach since late last spring. They've been killing every living thing that they find or turning them into Demons. They burn any human dwelling. Whole towns have been razed.

No one knows where they come from, or what their goal is, unless it's to kill everything. They are following a path up the Dragon's Spine and have almost reached Falcon's Spire. The king is calling in all reserves and has sent ambassadors to Talamh and Fèarmhar, requesting aid."

He paused, and then cleared his throat. "I very much fear that this is a repeat of the First Demon War."

Thomas gasped in surprise. His lessons included the history of the four kingdoms. The time of the First Demon War had come close to obliterating everything in the world and had caused the founding of Ard Ri, Talamh, Fasach and Fearmhar.

Wrung out by constant battle with the Ciardha Demons in the far reaches of time, the kings of the four lands had forged a pact with creatures of myth - Dragons. Once they had flown the skies, helping man to beat back the Dark. Their fiery breath had taken down hordes of misshapen creatures that served the Dark. They had been crucial in helping men win that war.

Now they were gone and no one knew why. The Dark had spent itself in skirmishes decade after decade, seeming to search for something it could not find.

The Duke, Captain Mathin and Gregory had fought together in the last skirmish twenty-five years ago, a skirmish that had almost been lost. Even then, the Dragons had not come.

Gregory moved his hand up the Dragon's Spine on the map and pointed to Red Dragon's Keep.

"Demons, minions of the Dark, are moving closer with each passing fortnight. I fear they will be here by early spring."

"But there aren't any Dragons to help us," exclaimed Thomas.

"I know, Lord Thomas. I've been looking through the records of the elder times, records that you haven't seen yet because they are so old, and I haven't found anything that might help us. There are only descriptions of what they did to arm their men and take care of the people during the battles that they fought.

There are some passages that are unbelievable, describing what the Dark did to people to turn them. I think perhaps it is time for you to read those accounts. Maybe you can see where I cannot. Perhaps your siblings and cousins can help, too," Gregory replied glumly, returning to the chair behind his desk.

Thomas sat frozen in shock. Gregory and Captain Mathin were the people he depended on to tell him what needed to be done. Without their advice, he felt helpless.

Captain Mathin stood and walked to the map. He clasped his hands behind his back, looking at it for several minutes. He finally reached out and traced the outline of Ard Ri with his right hand.

"Look here - do you see the pattern?" he asked. He pointed at the line of red glass beads.

"What pattern?" Gregory and Thomas spoke at the same time. "What do you see?" Thomas demanded as he leaned forward in his chair, then stood and walked over to stand next to the captain.

"Look at where the attacks have taken place. Look at the timing," Captain Mathin answered. "The Dark is following all of the rivers to every settlement. Makes sense, since people need water. Yet they are not crossing the water."

"The timing is the key," he said. "The attacks come at dusk when holders are returning to their cottages, very seldom at night. The question is why? What makes our people vulnerable then?"

Thomas stared at the map. Thoughtfully, he turned and resumed his seat. The fingers of his right hand picked at the tufts of thread on the arm of his chair. His left hand scrubbed restlessly at the knee of his trousers. The sweet cherry smell of Gregory's pipe smoke filled the air. Captain Mathin watched both of them.

"Well, people would be going home after working in the fields and might not be as aware of what's going on," Thomas said. "The sun has set, so there's not so much light. Do they ever attack during the day? Do they attack at night? Maybe there's something in the air? Why won't they cross the water?"

"All good questions," said Captain Mathin. "People who have fled to other Steadings might know the answers. I've sent men to talk to any survivors. They should be back in a day or two."

"Does anyone know where the Demons are coming from?" asked Thomas.

Sparks popped from one of the logs burning in the fireplace. Thomas flinched.

A knock sounded at the door. "Come in," Gregory called.

Lady Aeden pushed the door open, walked in, and closed the door behind her.

"Gentlemen, I've some news that you must hear." Her red-gold hair was pulled back into a tail. Trousers and a shirt in soft brown were covered with a forest green vest that fell to her knees. Well-worn black boots covered her feet and legs to mid-calf. Her sword hung in its scabbard from her belt.

Gregory, Captain Mathin and Thomas stood up as she entered the room. Impatient, she waved them back to their seats.

"Sit, please. Two of the scouts have returned. They spoke with a family that made it out of their Steading and fled north. They had to leave behind the elderlies."

Her voice caught on the last words and she swallowed, moved to the table sitting against the wall next to Gregory's desk and poured herself a mug of water. Her hand shook as she raised the mug to her mouth.

"It seems that the Dark only attacks at dawn and dusk, very rarely during the night, never during the day. As soon as the sun rose, the Dark fell back and broke off the chase. Why this is so is still a mystery. These are not the same Demons that you fought twenty-five years ago."

Captain Mathin broke the ensuing silence by clearing his throat. "Did the family try to cross any streams or rivers as they ran?"

"No", Aeden answered shortly. "They stayed on the west side of the Caladen."

"How many did they lose?" whispered Thomas.

"All told, they lost fifteen of their Steading," reported Aeden.

Thomas shook his head and closed his eyes. *What if that had been Owen and Breanna, or Cameron and Evan? I don't know that I could survive that.*

"Were any of the Dark killed?" asked Thomas. "We have got to figure out how to kill them," he exclaimed in frustrated confusion.

"I didn't think to ask," admitted Aeden. "Shall I have the scouts report to you?"

"Yes," said Thomas. She turned to leave. "Come back with them please, Lady Aeden. You know the questions to ask them."

He turned to the men as Aeden left the room.

"Gregory, Captain Mathin, do any of the very oldest records say how to kill these minions of the Dark? Are these like the ones that tried to take over the world in the founding times?"

Gregory and Captain Mathin looked at each other then turned toward the wall across from the fireplace where all the Keep records were shelved. Gregory walked down the wall to where the oldest records stood in ordered ranks.

"That would be around Record 113 I believe," said Captain Mathin. Gregory ran his fingers along the spines of the books of records. "Ah, here we are." He pulled the book marked 100 - 200 from the shelf. He blew dust from the top of the book. "A long time since this has been read. Let's see what it says."

Gregory walked over to the front of his desk and opened the record to its beginning. He turned the brittle pages, careful not to tear them. Captain Mathin and Thomas stood on either side of him and skimmed the pages as each was displayed.

"There," Thomas pointed at the page. "It mentions Demons."

The three bent closer to the record. "Nothing," Mathin breathed with a sigh. "I think this is after the first Demon war." The corners of Thomas's mouth turned down in disappointment and he frowned.

They straightened and looked at each other. Gregory shook his head in frustration. "I knew it couldn't be that easy." He closed the book and walked back to the shelf, replacing it carefully.

"Well, we're going to have to do it the hard way." He turned toward the two. "Thomas, you and the other younglings are going to have to help with this search. You can do it in the Library instead of the Solar, probably a candlemark before mid-meal. Mathin, will that leave enough time for them to get in weapons practice?"

"I'll make sure it does," Mathin replied.

Chapter 17

Marta mechanically put one foot in front of the other. Her arms and back ached fiercely from the heavy pack she shouldered, and the pack she carried for her granda. She stepped on another rock in the path and winced. The soles of her boots were never meant for this kind of travel and were wearing very thin.

The path rose before her, seeming a never ending ribbon of exhaustion, pain and hunger. This was the last pass the group had to climb before descending to the plateau that held Red Dragon's Keep.

Twenty of their number had died along the track. Their little band had been attacked almost nightly by Demons that she knew were trailing them. She tried to keep her granda in the center of the group, for safety's sake. It was becoming harder and harder to do as he lost what little strength he possessed and walked slower and slower. The rest of the group was restricted to her granda's slower pace. Two of the other elderlies had died and been buried along the way.

Word filtered down the line to stop for the night. "Your brothers found a clearing in the forest big enough to hold everyone," the young girls ahead of Marta told her.

In the late afternoon light, Marta looked back at the stragglers trudging up the path. *They'd better hurry. It's getting dark enough for the Demons to attack.*

She took her granda's arm and drew it over her shoulder. "Here, Granda. The ground is bad. Let me help you." She guided his faltering steps over the side of the track and into the little clearing. She walked with him over to a soaring giant of a tree and helped him slide down to sit at its base. She dropped to the ground next to him.

"Marta," her mother called across the clearing. "Can you come and help the others find places?"

Raina knelt over a pile of tinder that she was trying to light with the flint and steel Faolan had brought. The sparks fell on the wood-wool she'd gathered and a puff of smoke rose into the air. She bent down and gently blew on the smoldering nest. Tiny flames licked up the curls of wood. Carefully she moved the tinder to the kindling fire-bed that she'd prepared. The flames caught. She pushed herself up from her knees with a groan, wiping her hands on the legs of her trousers. She was as thin as her daughter, but not as tall.

Marta pushed herself wearily to her feet. *Why do I have to do it? I just want to curl up and not move.* She looked down at her sleeping granda. He was safe enough. She limped over to her mother. "Who needs help? Why do I have to do it?"

Raina looked at Marta with tired, drooping eyes. The dark red-brown hair she usually wore in a neat twist at the base of her neck had come loose and hair straggled over her shoulder. She swiped at it with a tired sigh and then reached back and pulled the pins out of her hair and let it tumble down her back. She looked at Marta and saw a young woman worn almost to the bone.

"I'm sorry, Marta. Because I don't have anyone else," she said quietly, rewinding her hair into its usual twist.

"I'm sorry too, Mama. I'm just so tired. I'm not even that afraid anymore," she said with a shake of her head. "Who should I help first?"

Raina looked around the clearing. There was very little conversation. Almost everyone had dropped their gear and simply sat where they'd stopped.

"Check with each family and ask if they have any food they can share. I've sent Kevin to get a bucket of water for the stew. I'm hoping that someone has some flour left for biscuits."

"Yes, Mama." Marta turned and trudged tiredly to each group. She asked the same question of each, "Do you have any flour? Mother wants to make biscuits. The stew should be ready for everyone soon." She moved from group to group, until she'd talked with all fifteen families that remained, gathering dried fruit and vegetables, some nuts and, the last family she talked to had flour. "Thank you," she murmured to everyone who contributed.

She made her way back to her mother at the center of the clearing. The fire was burning brightly now. The pots of water suspended over the fire were beginning to boil. "Here, Mama. I've got some dried vegetables and some fruit. I've also got a bag of flour."

"Thanks, Marta. Every little bit helps. Check on Granda, please," Raina said distractedly. She took the supplies that Marta had gathered and started adding them to pots. She set the bag of flour at the side of the fire-ring next to a bowl she would use to make the biscuits.

A creeping feeling of dread followed Marta back to her granda's resting place. The sun had set and dusk was swiftly giving way to the dark of night.

She took note of the eight men her father had assigned to stand guard. Most leaned on spears and watched the woods surrounding them with little attention. A few sat on boulders piled in a jumble to the left of the clearing from a rock slide in some distant past.

She scanned the trees that surrounded the clearing. The breeze that had been blowing in their faces all day had fallen still at dusk. She shut her eyes and listened intently. Faintly, she heard the snap of twigs as bodies moved through the forest.

"'Ware!" she shouted. "Something's coming!" She bent down and grabbed her granda's arm. "Hurry," she urged him out of his exhausted slumber, tugging on his arm. "To the fire," she shouted to the others. The guards jerked to alertness and lowered their spears.

Marta pulled her granda toward the fire as others clustered close around it. A guttural growl rumbled behind them as a Demon slipped between the guards and charged. Marta pulled her belt-knife from its sheath and whirled with a sob of fear and rage. The Demon leapt at her granda and landed on his back, taking him to the ground. He fell with a shout of fear.

With a scream of hatred, Marta jumped on the Demon's back and drove her knife between its ribs into its heart. The monster stiffened and went still. She rolled off of its back and pushed desperately against its bulk, trying to uncover her granda.

Demons attacked the outer ring of guards, slashing through spear shafts and ducking under swinging swords. Several slipped through and leaped toward the center of the camp where everyone clustered. Men and women stepped in front of the group, thrusting with swords and punching with the butts of quarterstaffs.

With a bellow of rage, Faolan attacked the Demons closest to his daughter and father. He struck with his broadsword, separating a head from a body and ending with a cut through the spine of the next. He dropped his sword and fell down on his knees next to Marta, shoving the body of the Demon off of his father. Grief clenched his heart and twisted his face as he saw what lay under the Demon.

Marta screamed and clutched at Faolan. Her granda was dead. The Demon's claws had gone entirely through his body, killing him instantly. Faolan turned to Marta and folded her into his arms. He looked around the clearing as tears rolled down his face.

The Demons were dead. Their bodies were scattered around the clearing. Six holders lay dead, including his father and two children. Faolan stood and pulled Marta up with him, looking for Raina and his sons. He saw them across the clearing, pulling their swords free from a Demon's mutilated body.

Marta was panting for breath. Tears drenched her eyes, making it difficult to see. She dashed them from her eyes with trembling hands and looked toward the forest.

A large black body stood on a branch half way up the tall leafless tree where her granda had been resting. The firelight reflected from its large blood-red eyes. Tall appendages framed its head, ending in hooks curving over its skull. As she watched, something stretched out from the sides of its body and the appendages became wings.

Whatever it was fell from the branch and flew away through the trees, twisting and turning to avoid collision with the trunks that stood in its way.

The survivors pulled the eleven Demon bodies out of the clearing and down the track back toward the Steading. They piled them in the center of the road. Arrows wrapped with cloth and lit at the camp's main fire flew into the pile. The bodies ignited and sent a choking grey-black cloud of smoke rising into the night air, drifting slowly away from the campsite.

Families buried their dead. Faolan stood at the head of his father's grave, Raina, Marta, Jaiman and Kevin standing at its side, arms wrapped around each other. "He was a good man and loving father. You'll be missed, Da."

He looked beyond the grave to the people he was responsible for, grieving for their sorrow. Raising his voice so everyone could hear, he told them what needed to be done. "I'd like to stay here tomorrow, but I don't think we can. We'll leave at mid-morning and stop early to rest. The sooner we reach Red Dragon's Keep, the safer we'll be. Get what sleep you can."

He and his family walked away from his father's final resting place.

Chapter 18

Thomas turned another page in the record book that he was searching. Somewhere in here there *had* to be a report or evidence or *something* to tell them how to fight the Dark. He and the boys and Breanna had been searching every record that Gregory sent them.

Cameron sat next to him, his head in his hand supported by his elbow on the table. He flipped page after page, not really paying attention. Evan and Owen sat on the opposite side of the table, each reading a book. A pile of ten more records sat stacked at the end of the table.

Breanna had gone to get a skully to bring them some food and drinks to share before mid-meal. The warmth from the fire burning in the fireplace across the room didn't reach the table. The Library was cold.

Cameron suddenly sat up straight. "Thomas, look at this! I think it's important!"

Thomas, Evan, and Owen crowded around Cameron as he pointed toward a drawing in the record.

The drawing showed what looked like a broken piece of a talisman. It was a triangle with four gems placed from the center to the rim on a raised bar set on the right side. Runes and words were inscribed on either side of the triangle, some of them missing because of the broken edges. *Cumhacht ar Draigoini* labeled the picture. Thomas shivered as the boys gasped. *Power of Dragons.*

Thomas put his hand on Evans shoulder. "Go get Gregory and Captain Mathin as quick as you can." He pushed Evan toward the door.

He nudged Cameron out of his chair and began to read the description in the record.

"The Cumhacht ar Draigoini gives the bearer power to call the Dragons. Through it, the Dragons are required to do whatever the bearer desires. It has the power to kill the Dragons."

Instructions on how to use the talisman followed its description.

The record continued after the instructions. *"Following the last war with the Ciardha Demon, the Cumhacht ar Draigoini was broken by the Rune of Getal into five pieces and hidden in five strongholds throughout the kingdom of Ard Ri. This was done to protect humans as well as Dragons, removing the temptation of complete power. Should the Dragons be needed in the future, all five pieces must be reunited with the incantation of Xarroon. The Talisman cannot be destroyed. It is protected with runes inscribed on its rim by the first mage council when Dragons were created."*

Thomas sat back in astonishment.

Quick footsteps sounded in the hallway and Gregory and Captain Mathin hurried into the room followed by Evan.

"What have you found?" barked Captain Mathin.

"Cameron may have found the reason that the Demons keep attacking," Thomas whispered. "Here. Read this." He slid the book across the table to the two men, careless of its age.

The men bent over the book to read the passage. As they finished reading, Gregory reached out to brace himself on the back of the chair closest to him and slowly sat. Captain Mathin sank onto the bench that Evan had been using.

Both men looked at Thomas, as stunned as he was. Slowly the disbelief wore off.

"Do you think that one of the pieces is hidden here?" Thomas asked quietly.

Both Gregory and Mathin shook their heads.

"There's no way to tell," Gregory croaked. He cleared his throat. "The only thing to be done is a search, a quiet search, done by those who are completely trustworthy."

Captain Mathin frowned sternly at all of them. "Not one word about this is to be spoken outside of this room. We don't know whom we can trust. Boys, do you understand?"

All of them nodded in agreement.

"You can't even talk about it when you think you're alone. We should meet again tomorrow, just us, to talk about this," Thomas ordered. "Maybe we can figure out where it is, if it's even in the Keep."

"Aye. No one speaks of this. Swear on it." Captain Mathin held out his right hand. One by one, the boys and Gregory put their right hands on top of his, Thomas last of all.

As their hands fell away, Breanna returned with a pitcher and cups. A skully followed her with a basket of rolls. Thomas reached across the table and closed the record book. Gregory picked it up. "I'll just return this to my office," he said and strode out of the room. Captain Mathin nodded his head at Thomas and followed Gregory out.

"Here's some hot chocolate and rolls," Breanna said. "Let's eat!"

§ § §

Thomas worried at the problem of what he began to call *the talisman search* into the night. He checked every single room and passage in the Keep, mentally running the locations through his mind. He fell into exhausted sleep just as dawn light faintly brightened behind the shutters at his window.

He woke three candlemarks later when his chamberlain entered the room with a pitcher of hot water. Simon carried it across the room and set it next to the bowl sitting on the commode. He turned to the fireplace and added logs to the embers. The wood smoked briefly and then burst into flames.

"My Lord, Gregory was asking for you. He requested that you meet him in his office when you are ready," he said as he gathered Thomas's clothes from the day before.

Thomas sat up in bed and yawned hugely as he stretched himself awake. He swung his legs from under the blankets to the side of his bed and rested his elbows on his knees. He was still tired. His heart sped up as he remembered the talisman. He clenched his hands into fists.

"Thanks, Simon. I'll find him as soon as I can."

"I'll let him know." Simon pulled the door closed as he left the room.

Thomas stood stretched with weariness and yawned again. He quickly pulled on clothes and shoved his feet into boots. He rubbed his hand over his chin, prickly with the beginnings of a beard. *Finally. I'll have to start shaving soon.*

He walked to his weapons rack and buckled on his sword. He'd decided to wear it all the time after the squires' treachery. A sudden thought blazed in his mind and he froze. *What about the secret passage?* He hadn't been in there since he'd listened to the scouts report to Gregory. He stood motionless in thought for what felt like ages. He decided that he'd need to check every passage when he had time.

Thomas made his way to the great hall and served himself breakfast. He wolfed it down, and then went to find Gregory.

Gregory was in his office, reading the Dragon talisman record that he'd set on the bookstand next to the windows behind his desk. He turned as Thomas entered the room.

"Good morning, Gregory. Simon said that you wanted to talk to me."

"I did, my Lord. I've been worrying at the question all night. Your weapons practice will take up most of the morning and I don't think it's wise to break your routine. I think we should meet today after mid-meal. We need to make some decisions quickly about how to proceed."

Thomas sighed. "I agree. I tossed and turned all night. Dreams of Dragons chasing me kept waking me up." He snorted. "I've never had *that* kind of dream before." He shook his head. "Please tell the boys and Captain Mathin that we'll meet after mid-meal in the Library. I'd better get to practice."

Gregory patted him on the shoulder. "You're doing well, Thomas. Just think about training and nothing else, if you can. We'll see you at mid-meal."

Thomas worked up a sweat as he swung his sword against the pells, then reversed and brought his dagger across to attack. His weapons thudded again and again against the wooden target. He would lose himself in the rhythm and then suddenly remember the talisman. His body clenched and he'd lose the smooth flow of the practice.

He finally stepped back and wiped the sweat from his forehead, sheathed his sword at his side and guided his dagger into its scabbard.

"My Lord, you're not done with the pells yet," shouted the sergeant in charge of squire practice. He strode toward Thomas from the far end of the practice field.

"I'm sorry, sergeant," Thomas said. "I'm not feeling well. I think I need to see Moirra."

The sergeant frowned as he reached Thomas. He took one look at Thomas's glassy eyes and waved him toward the Tower. "Very well, my Lord. We'll see you tomorrow."

Thomas nodded and trudged away from the practice field. He stomach rolled in protest. *Maybe I really am getting sick and this isn't just dodging practice. I don't want anything to eat.*

He made his way through the kitchen and into the great hall. He turned to the stairs and saw Cameron, Evan and Owen trying to walk casually toward him along the wall. He almost laughed and hoped he didn't look as tense as they did. Silently they met at the foot of the staircase.

"Did any of you eat?" he asked in a low voice.

The others shook their heads.

"Come on. It will look suspicious if we don't eat. Breanna will notice for sure."

He turned toward the sideboard and took a small bowl of soup and a piece of bread. The boys did the same. They made their way to the head table and took their seats. Breanna rushed into the room, grabbed a bowl and bread as well, and joined them.

Thomas ate slowly. His stomach refused to settle. He put the bowl down. "What have you been doing, Breanna?"

"I've been working with the new colt from the white mare that Father bought. He's a beauty. I've already got him following me around the paddock," Breanna smiled and dipped her bread in the soup. She took a big bite.

"Pretty soon I'm going to put a blanket across his back and teach him to lift his feet on command," she said around the food.

Thomas frowned. "You be careful, Breanna. Don't get hurt."

Breanna grinned. "Don't worry. All of the horses like me, Thomas. It's almost like I can read what they are going to do before they do it."

"Still," Thomas muttered. "Just be careful."

Breanna punched him in the arm. "I will be," she said.

He glanced down the table. The others had finished their soup and were waiting for him. He got up and walked over to them.

"Meet me in the Library. Leave about five minutes apart," he said quietly. He made his way to the stairs and started up.

Captain Mathin and Gregory joined them as they reached the Library. Captain Mathin carried the book. He placed it on the table. Everyone looked tired.

"I think we need to include Breanna in this," Thomas blurted out. "It's really hard to keep anything from her and she might have some good ideas. Lady Aeden, too. She has magic and can help," he finished.

"I agree," Captain Mathin nodded his head. "We need all the help we can get. The only way we will find that amulet is to do a search room by room and corridor by corridor. Gregory, could you have a skully find Lady Aeden and Lady Breanna? Tell them to meet us here."

Lady Aeden and Breanna joined them a few minutes later. The skully had found them in the stable paddock, just starting to work with the colt.

"What is it?" asked Lady Aeden.

Breanna looked apprehensively at the boys. "What have you found?" she quavered.

Captain Mathin waved at Cameron. Cameron looked at him and jerked his head around toward Breanna.

"We might have found the reason the Demons are here," he said in a rush. "There's a talisman that was broken into five pieces. It can control the Dragons." His voice rose steadily as he spoke.

Lady Aeden went white in shock. "What?" she gasped. "Of course," she muttered.

Breanna stood mute, her eyes huge. She shook off her shock and ran to the table. She braced her hands on its top, leaning toward Cameron. "Do you know where it is?" she cried.

Cameron shook his head. "It doesn't say where, just that it was hidden," he responded.

Breanna slumped into a chair. "This doesn't help at all," she wailed.

Lady Aeden moved to her and put a calming hand on her shoulder.

"Yes, it does," Aeden told her. "These amulets are what the Dark and its minions, the High Sorcerer and the Demons, are searching for like a swarm of locusts. If they can control the Dragons, they will kill them. Without the Dragons, the kingdom is lost. We can't win without them.

I didn't know that Dragons *could* be controlled. We *must* find those pieces. Show me what you've found," Aeden demanded.

Captain Mathin pushed the record book across the table to her.

Quickly she read the passage and studied the drawing. A frown marred her forehead. "I swear I've seen this somewhere. I just can't remember where." She shook her head in frustration and gently closed the book.

"Captain Mathin, Gregory, I would suggest that you hide this record. No one must know about this, at least not yet." Aeden spoke quietly and carefully.

Thomas looked grimly at everyone around the table. "I had a horrible thought this morning. What if one of the amulets is at Falcon's Spire and it falls to the Demons?"

Everyone reacted, inhaling sharply at the thought.

"By the Three," Captain Mathin exclaimed. "We'd better assume that they will find one there if they take the Spire. It makes sense. I'll bet there's one here, one at Falcon's Spire, another at Windward Stronghold and somewhere in Cathair Ri. Where would the last one be hidden?"

"With the Dragons," Lady Aeden whispered.

Chapter 19

Hugo, the stableman, called to Jalyn from the open door to the delivery yard and kitchen garden. Heat from the kitchen flowed out the door and he took several steps back.

"Mistress Jalyn, I have a message for you." His gap-toothed smile belied the ugly glitter in his eyes.

Shaking her head, Jalyn bustled to the door, her enormous hips swaying. Frowning, she stepped out of the door onto the porch and berated Hugo. "How dare you come to the kitchen," she hissed in anger. "We should only meet at night."

"Shut your gob, you fat scum. I've been sent by the High Draiolc Mannan. He 'requests' a meeting tonight. Come to the stable at the eleventh candlemark."

Turning on his heel, he stepped down the rest of the stairs and strode out of the yard.

Panic shot through Jalyn and her stomach contracted painfully. She turned and waddled back into the kitchen.

She had nothing to report. Everything she tried had fallen short. She had worked the spells she knew to make someone clumsy or forgetful, hoping that a deadly accident would result. She'd poisoned the food and drink to no avail. Now the Duke and Duchess were gone and she wouldn't have another chance. Plans skittered through her mind.

She decided to be bold and demand a spell that would kill all of the Arachs at once.

§ § §

The moon rode the sky like a ghost ship under full sail. At the eleventh candlemark, Jalyn moved as quietly as she could from the kitchen to the stable. Darkness made shadows feel cold and sinister. She swayed along the side of the Keep, scuffing through the frozen leaves exposed after the last scant snowfall melted during the warmer temperatures of day. Winter was coming.

Reaching the stable, Jalyn pushed the door open along its sliding track. She slid it closed behind her and hurried to the tack-room, the only enclosed area in the building.

The large room was filled with saddles on saddle-racks, bridles hanging from pegs, halters and other stable equipment stacked on shelves. A very faint red glow filled the room, its source not visible.

In the darkest corner, a creature from the halls of hell stood in utter stillness. Clothed in black, tall and thin, its face and hands were as white as chalk. White hair crowning a corpselike skull, Mannan, the High Draiolc - darkest of all sorcerers - waited.

Hugo, for all of his bravado, stood as far from the sorcerer as he could get. His eyes shifted from side to side, as if seeking a way out of what he'd agreed to do.

A sound like the rattling and rubbing of large insect wings filled the air.

"What have you done to carry out my orders?" rasped Mannan's voice.

"My lord, greatest of sorcerers, I have tried everything that I know," Jalyn whined. "Poisons, spells to entangle feet and hands, spells of forgetfulness. Every one of them has been fruitless. I don't know what else to try. I don't understand why nothing is working when it should have. Give me a spell that will kill them all," she demanded.

The rubbing whine of insect wings grew louder as the temperature in the room began to rise.

"The taste of Dragon magic saturates the very stones of this Keep. Have you not seen or felt any of it while you have been here?" Mannan's low voice snarled.

"No, my Lord. I've felt nothing. I've checked as much as I safely can with both spell and scrying. There has been *nothing*," Jalyn whispered in a shaking voice, finally realizing she'd made a mistake.

The temperature in the tack-room soared, mirroring Mannan's anger. With a gesture of his hand, Jalyn was thrown from her feet and pinned to the floor. Another gesture instantly muffled her agonized scream of pain and fear.

"Woman, you have failed yet again. Your value is decreasing by the moment," he growled. She shrieked again as he closed his hand into a fist and twisted. Blood began to seep from Jalyn's ears. "The only reason I don't kill you now and drink your blood is because you are too entwined in the life of this place. You *will* carry out my orders."

"Lord, Lord! I swear I will do whatever you want of me. Please, please!" Jalyn choked in terror on her own blood.

§ § §

Hugo shrank against the wood of the wall. His fear was growing beyond anything he'd ever known. He hadn't recognized the power of the sorcerer to whom he had pledged his soul in exchange for a small portion of that power. His ragged pants grew damp as a hot stream of pee trickled down his leg. He began to tremble uncontrollably.

Mannan slowly turned toward him. Hugo hurriedly dropped his eyes.

"Have *you* at least carried out my orders?" asked Mannan.

"Lord, I shaved the wooden pins that hold the wagon wheels to the axles. They will not last to the capital. I put weevils in the supplies and pin holes in the water barrels. The barrels should be dry by Great Falls and unfillable." mumbled Hugo with a quaver in his voice.

"Good. At least the ambush that I have arranged should produce results," Mannan snarled.

"Move this trash back to the kitchen. I will give you instructions to pass to her. Should she fail again, the instructions to you include killing her and disposing of the body. You will find another minion to take her place." Mannan waved in disgust toward the weeping woman huddled on the floor in front of him.

"Yes, Lord."

Mannan whirled away, his cloak billowing. He raised his arms toward the ceiling. A glowing rune grew in the air as he moved his hands in a complicated pattern. A step toward the rune, and the sorcerer was gone. The rune-glow slowly faded. The room was plunged into darkness.

Hugo shuddered and dropped to his knees. Minutes passed as he shook in reaction. He crabbed over to the hysterically weeping Jalyn and jerked her up to her knees. He slapped her across the face. "Come on, you halfwit. Get yourself under control. You need to get cleaned up," he muttered hoarsely.

§ § §

Thomas pulled on old trousers, a shirt and warm tunic. He belted his sword to his waist and stepped into soft leather boots. He ran down the stairs and turned toward Gregory's office. He and Gregory had agreed to meet as soon as Thomas awakened to plan the search for the Dragon amulet. A shout of rage stopped him in his tracks as he turned through the doorway.

Gregory's face was red with anger. One of the cooks stood in front of him, twisting his apron with shaking hands, shivering with fear.

"Sir, I'm sorry. I don't know where the flour disappeared to or when the last load of grain spoiled. I checked myself and all was in order ten days ago. No one was near the granary or the storeroom as far as I know," the distraught cook choked out. "The spoilage is too quick to be fungus.

"I'm not blaming you, man. I'm appalled that it's not been noticed until now. This means that we have another traitor in our midst and we must ferret him out or face disaster," Gregory growled in a low voice.

"Tell no one what you've found. We don't need a panic. Check all of the other supplies yourself and report back. I want your ideas on what needs to be done. Be quick."

The cook nodded his head. "Yes sir." He turned, bowed to Thomas and scurried out of the room.

Thomas stood frozen and looked at Gregory. Gregory shook his head and motioned Thomas into the room.

"Close the door. We don't need any more gossip." He turned toward the large window that looked out on the south approach to the Keep and started to pace, his hands clasped behind his back.

Thomas closed the door quietly and quickly, after glancing both ways down the hall. No one lurked or lingered. He turned back to Gregory. "What do we do?" he asked.

"First, don't say a word to another soul. If they know that supplies are short, there could well be a panic." Gregory turned to face Thomas, running his hand distractedly through his hair. "I'm sorry, my Lord. This should never have progressed so far."

"Gregory, this isn't your fault. It's the fault of whoever is stealing from this Keep, from the people who depend on us for their very lives. How we catch him is the question," Thomas spoke slowly. He was thinking furiously. "This may be bigger than we know. I've heard things during training and clean-up that make some sense now."

Gregory grabbed his shoulder. "What have you heard?" He gave Thomas a quick shake, released his shoulder and held up his hand. "Wait, I'll send for Captain Mathin. He should be involved in this."

Turning to his desk, he jotted a quick note on a scrap of paper he found there, then strode to the door and shouted across the hall, "Jago, front!"

Short and plump, Jago, Gregory's clerk, charged out of his room across the hall. "Master, what do you need?"

Gregory thrust the folded paper into his hands. "Find Captain Mathin as quick as you can. This is urgent."

"Yes sir." Jago turned and jogged down the hallway.

Gregory hurried back into the room. He scrubbed his hands on his cheeks, shook his head and moved to sit behind his desk. "Please, sit, Lord Thomas."

Thomas hastily took a seat on one of the chairs in front of Gregory's desk. He turned toward the doorway as he heard booted feet striding down the corridor. "Captain Mathin, we have a problem," he said as the captain swung into the room, moving fast.

"What's wrong?" Mathin demanded, making his way to the other chair.

Gregory told him about the missing supplies and spoiled grain. "It's too quick for mold or fungus," he finished.

Mathin turned to Thomas. "What have you heard?"

Thomas leaned forward and put his elbows on his knees, his hands clasped between his legs. "There's been muttering among the skullies about something in the undercroft, something that has them terrified. They mutter about strange smells from there and the stables. Even Cameron has heard tales of ghosts under the Tower. Has anyone said anything to you about skullies disappearing?"

"No, no one has said anything." Mathin turned cool grey eyes on Gregory, one eyebrow raised.

"No one has spoken to me about missing skullies," Gregory said with a frown.

Thomas rubbed his chin as he sat back. "I think it was last week that I heard two of the soldiers talking about something they had heard at the market. The villagers are telling tales of food rotting in their cellars and going missing from storage."

Captain Mathin surged to his feet. "This is the work of some foul traitor or mage who is bent on betraying us. Who would or could do this without anyone noticing?"

Thomas shook his head. "We need Lady Aeden."

Gregory stood and walked to the door. "I'll send Jago to fetch her."

§ § §

The sun had passed mid-morning when Jago returned with Lady Aeden. She had just returned from a scouting patrol. Gregory dismissed him with a curt order to get his mid-meal.

"Can you discover if there has been spell-work done in the Keep?" demanded Captain Mathin of Aeden. "If you can't, do you know someone who can?"

Aeden gave them a puzzled look. "Why? What's happened?"

"We think someone has tainted the food stores and skullies are missing. It's happened within the past fortnight."

"I can certainly try to see if someone has left traces," Aeden declared. "Who told you? How many people know?"

"The undercook reported it to me this morning. The only others who know are in this room, and my clerk, Jago," Gregory told her.

He spoke slowly and thoughtfully. "I'm wondering what's in the undercroft that has the skullies spooked. The only things down there are the well and storage for supplies. I'll order a search. Captain Mathin, can you please provide men to do that?"

"Of course," said Mathin. "Thomas, if you would come with me, I think we should do this together. Gregory and Lady Aeden, you should investigate the tainting and disappearance of the food."

"I'll get that started now," Gregory agreed. "Good luck, gentlemen. Lady Aeden, if you'd follow me?"

Chapter 20

Scout Leader Quinn, rail thin and very strong, pulled his sword from the disgusting gray skinned, black furred body. The smell was horrible, ammonia and acid combined. He gagged. His black hair was matted with Demon blood.

His squad of twelve had been sent out four miles into the mountains south and west of Red Dragon's Keep, searching for any incursion by the Ciardha Demons. They had found it. Two of his men were dead, throats ripped out and disemboweled by the six hell-spawn they had encountered. Those six bodies lay smoking and bubbling on the forest floor, but at enormous cost. Every one of his men had slashes and bites on arms, legs, heads, and torsos. He prayed that those wounds wouldn't fester, but he had a terrible feeling about this.

Light snow drifted down from a gray sky. Quinn squinted his dark brown eyes and glanced around the small clearing. Leafless trees raised brittle branches to claw at the tattered clouds. More snow was on the way; he could smell it. He shivered. *What else is on the way?*

He knelt down on one knee to examine the hell-spawn he had killed.

Its body was elongated with a stubby tail and four legs armed with razor sharp claws on five toes. Teeth two inches long filled its huge jaws like those of the razor fish that lived in the mighty rivers that emptied into the sea along the coast. Large eyes with pupils like those of a cat dominated its head.

Huge eyes, serrated teeth, and razor sharp claws, he mused. *A very small brain; this was made for killing, for war.* Short, coarse black hair covered a grey, thick, tough hide.

Shaking his head, he wiped his sword on the dead Demon, then stood and turned to Ben, his second-in-command. "Send someone back to the Keep. Ask for a wagon for the bodies of our fallen. We need one of the wise-women to treat the wounded. Ask for Moirra. She's the best. We need more troops. Quick now, we don't know how many more Demons are out here."

"Aye sir, I'll get right on it," Ben said, then drew a shuddering breath. "This goes beyond anything I've ever seen, or imagined for that matter. Have you seen such, sir?"

"No, Ben, I've not." Quinn clasped Ben's shoulder. "I've heard tales from the Great War of beasts such as these, but never seen them. Get going. I'll set the least wounded to making camp. We need a defensive perimeter." Ben hurried off to find a messenger.

$ $ $

The watch guards at the gates stiffened to alertness. A small cloud of dust was billowing up along the approach to the Keep. The private on duty shouted down to the guardhouse. "Sergeant, rider approaching from the south!"

The sergeant stepped out of the guardhouse and charged up the stone steps of the watchtower.

He gained the top of the rampart and leaned out to watch the dust cloud. He grunted, and then barked, "Man the gates, that's a courier." Two of the gate company moved briskly to comply.

The black horse carrying the courier was covered in sweat and lather. Foam depended from its gaping mouth. As it raced to the end of the drawbridge over the dry moat in front of the Keep wall, its heart burst and it stumbled, went to its knees and flipped over onto its side, dead in that instant.

Its body landed within inches of the tumbling courier. The courier flew through the air, landed hard and slid out onto the bridge. The gate guards ran out across the bridge, pulled the courier up to his feet and supported him under each arm through the inner Keep gate. The watch sergeant hurried to them and the courier gasped out, "Tell the Lord that Falcon's Spire has fallen. The Ciardha Demons have arrived and slain all left within her walls."

He slumped in the guards' arms as his mind spiraled into unconsciousness.

Chapter 21

Chaos reigned.

The message from Falcon's Spire arrived as Thomas and Captain Mathin were planning the search of the undercroft in the Library.

The news sent a bolt of fear and dread through everyone in the Tower, and in the town as the news spread.

The scouts' messenger arrived, reporting the Demon attack on his patrol, requesting more men and a wagon for the dead.

As the sun marched toward the western horizon, a soldier from the Duke's supply train rode through the gates. Tired and gaunt, he slid down from the bare back of the farm horse he was riding. He looked like a farmer.

The guards at the gate rushed to his side, pulling his arms across their shoulders. The sergeant-in-charge recognized him. "What's happened? Why are you back," he demanded.

"I need to report to Captain Mathin," the exhausted man mumbled, tired beyond words.

"Private, go alert Captain Mathin. Find Lord Thomas, too. I'll bring him into the great hall," ordered the watch sergeant. He sent the remaining private back to the gates, then draped the soldier's arm across his own shoulders. They hobbled across the forecourt and made their way, one step at a time, up the stairs and into the great hall.

The sergeant helped the soldier stumble to the nearest table, shoving the bench out from under it with his foot. The soldier folded onto the bench and pillowed his head on his arms on the table. The sergeant shouted to a skully to bring water and soup.

Captain Mathin and Thomas descended the stairs into the great hall. They strode to the table where the scout was sipping slowly from a mug. A bowl of soup sat on the table in front of him. They slid onto the bench on the other side of the table.

Captain Mathin angled his head in query. "What happened to you? You look completely done in."

"Captain, Lord Thomas." The soldier raised bleary, glassy eyes to look at both of them. "I have desperate news. Three of the wagons failed. Most of the pins holding the wheels to the axles were shaved and broke so the wheels fell off. All of the spares were shaved, too. Most of the food spoiled.

We were ambushed at Great Falls three weeks out from Red Dragon's Keep. Lord Tom and Lord Jeremy and Lady Jenni and Lady Anne fought like h...heck, but there were too many men. One of them was that traitor, Garan. We tried to save them, but there were too many and they cut us down. All the other men were killed."

He shook his head and, picking up the bowl of soup, took a small sip. "I got knocked on the head and couldn't get up again. I watched them pull the Lords from their saddles and tie them up. The women tried to keep fighting, but Lady Jenni was cut pretty bad and knocked from her saddle. Lady Anne jumped down from her horse to help, but she was hit on the back of the head."

Thomas gasped in shock and fear. The soldier looked up at him in sympathy.

"All of them were tied up and thrown over horses that the ambushers brought out of the trees. They took all of our horses and everything they could carry. I don't know where they went!" His voice rose as he finished the telling.

"It's taken me almost three weeks to get back. I travelled slow during the day, trying to look like a farmer. I stole some clothes from one of the holdings.

I hid in the trees at sunrise and sunset. There are Demon bands moving everywhere during those times. I was afraid there were more traitors along the way. I finally stole a farmer's horse about three days out from the Keep and came as fast as I could."

"Good job," murmured Captain Mathin. "Sergeant - both of you - this news stays at this table, understand?" Both men nodded. "Take him to the barracks and let him sleep his journey out."

"Yes, sir," the sergeant said. He patted the soldier on the arm. "Come on. I'll get you settled." The exhausted man was soon asleep in the barracks.

Thomas sat mute and in shock. He couldn't think. His parents were gone.

Captain Mathin sat as still as a statue. Abruptly he stood, pushing the bench back from the table. Thomas stood hastily as well. "I need to put together a search party. We leave tomorrow. I'm sorry, lad. This comes first."

"I agree, Captain. Do what you think best." Thomas mumbled. His voice hoarse with fear, he called to a skully and sent him off to find a courier. He needed to send a report to the King, relaying his horrendous news and warning him of the threat along the Dragon's Spine.

§ § §

The next morning Thomas stood on the steps of the Tower, arms folded across his chest, cloak stirring in the errant zephyrs that swirled over the walls. Scowling, he watched as one hundred of the Keep's defenders saddled horses and loaded supplies into wagons waiting in the forecourt.

Sparks flew as iron shod hooves slid on flagstone. Shouts and noise filled the air. Twenty of the soldiers would turn to the southwest to reinforce the scouts who had been attacked. The rest of the soldiers would follow Captain Mathin on the hunt for Thomas's parents, aunt and uncle.

Captain Mathin ascended the stairs and stood next to him, watching the column assemble. Snow sifted down from a leaden sky to dampen cloaks and hoods.

"Lord Thomas, the men should be ready to leave in the next half candlemark. We've not had time to search for the traitor, nor what lurks in the undercroft. I'm sorry, but I must go and try to find the Duke and Duchess."

"Captain Mathin, are you sure that this is a wise course? Shouldn't we send scouts and rovers out to search?" asked Thomas. "With Demons this close, do we have enough men to defend the Keep?"

Captain Mathin looked at him long and hard. "Lad, there's no help for it. You've learned a tremendous amount in the past months. You've got the basics down and the rest is just flourishes. Lady Aeden and Gregory can guide you now as well as I can. I'm leaving you enough men to see the Keep safe. The longer I wait, the colder the Duke's trail."

Thomas dropped his eyes and stared at the ground. The silence stretched. He shook his head and looked up at Mathin.

"Please find them," he whispered, his eyes bright with unshed tears.

Mathin put a hand on his shoulder. "I will, lad. That I promise," he said.

He shouted for a stableman to bring his horse. The stableman led a dark sorrel warhorse to the stairs, its coat gleaming with sweat. It was huge, larger than the Duke's charger. Mathin put his foot in the stirrup while still standing on the second stair. He swung himself up into the saddle. He reined the horse around to face Thomas and saluted him. "Lord Thomas, we'll find them."

The horse spun on his hocks at a move of Mathin's leg and trotted to the front of the column of riders. The riders began to move out of the forecourt and onto the road to Great Falls. Wagons rumbled as they followed the riders. Soon the forecourt was empty.

Glumly, Thomas shook his head, turned and climbed the stairs into the Keep.

Gregory and Lady Aeden met him at the doors. They glanced at each other.

"Lord Thomas, I've gathered men to search the undercroft and dungeons. We should do this now," she said.

Gregory moved to block sight of him from the hall. "Lord, we think we know who has betrayed us," he said in a low voice. "Lady Aeden has felt something odd for the past fortnight and traced it back to its maker. We knew last night, but," he gestured toward the departing column, "getting them ready to leave took precedence." He turned back to Thomas. "There are several people. What do you want me to do?"

Thomas frowned and glanced around to see who might be listening. No one was close enough to overhear. "Gather them quietly and put them in one of the storerooms in chains. Two guards inside and two guards outside of the room. No chances for escape, do you understand?"

"I do, Lord. Just so you aren't surprised, one of them is Jalyn, the head cook. She's the one responsible for the spoiled grain and damaged supplies."

Thomas gasped in outrage as his eyes widened and his face paled. He shook his head in bewilderment. He would never have suspected her. He had known Jalyn his entire life. She had always been a fantastic cook and had been treated as almost one of the family.

What a perfect position to keep track of everything that was going on in the Keep, as well as having access to the means to kill people and betray the Duke, he thought in despair.

He turned abruptly to Lady Aeden. "Let's go. The sooner we find out what's down there, the quicker we can deal with it."

Calling to the men, Lady Aeden started toward the guardroom to the right of the main hall with its access to the undercroft. Abruptly she stopped. "My Lord, we should bring the other members of your family to keep them safe. Who knows what might be loose in the Keep." she spoke quietly.

Thomas nodded and called to the closest of the assembled men. "Corporal, please go to the family's rooms and ask Cameron, Evan, Owen & Breanna to dress quickly and warmly and meet here in the great hall within the quarter candlemark." The corporal turned and hurried toward the steps to the second floor.

Thomas looked grimly at Gregory. "We'll deal with the traitors as soon as we're done in the undercroft. If something happens, kill them. We cannot have them at our backs while we fight the Ciardha Demon."

Gregory blanched. "Yes, my Lord." He bowed with respect, and maybe a little fear.

§ § §

Cameron, Evan, Owen and Breanna ran down the stairs to the great hall. They had thrown on thick wool trousers and shirts as well as tunics that fell to mid-thigh. Owen wore his long knife in a sheath that was belted to his waist. They stumbled to a stop as they reached the bottom of the stairs. All of them had red eyes from crying at the news of their parents' kidnapping.

The room was filled with men-at-arms bearing swords and crossbows. Low murmuring filled the air. Thomas turned from his discussion with Lady Aeden and Gregory and beckoned them over to the group.

"Owen. Good. You're armed," Thomas said. Lady Aeden extended three shorter knives in sheaths to him. Thomas took the knives and looked at Evan, Cameron and Breanna. "All of us need to be armed, just in case." He handed a knife to each one of them. "Thread these onto your belts. We're going to the undercroft to find out why all of the skullies are afraid to go down there."

"Lady Aeden, if you'd stay with us?" She nodded assent. "The captain will lead the first half of the men down. We'll all go next." He gestured at his siblings, cousins and Lady Aeden. "Sergeant Padric will follow with the rest of the men."

The first group of soldiers moved to the wide staircase that descended from the hallway between the great hall and kitchen. They spread themselves out, two soldiers close together at the front of the line, then several steps between each of the rest.

Lady Aeden moved silently after the last of the first group. Thomas followed her. "Everyone, keep up with me but don't bunch together. We need to be able to move around if there's an attack." They started down the staircase.

Breanna began to quietly cry. Thomas slowed down and put an arm around her and Evan. "It's all right to cry. Just don't let it distract you," he whispered to them. "Okay," they whispered back in chorus.

What am I doing? I don't know what we might face. Maybe I should leave the other kids behind.

A very, very low moan shook his bones. The hairs on the back of his neck stood straight up. Everyone froze on the staircase.

Why hasn't anyone told us about this? Why hasn't someone talked about missing skullies?

"Don't stop," he ordered.

The line of soldiers began to move slowly and as quietly as possible down the stairs.

The rough stone of the wall caught the fabric of Thomas's tunic as he slid against it. The putrid smell of rotting meat filled the air as they descended. The first soldiers hit the bottom of the stairs and moved left and right, swords leading, sweeping the area for danger. Another eerie moan shivered through the undercroft.

"What *is* that, Lady Aeden?" Thomas whispered his question.

"I'm not sure, Lord. It sounds like a seleigh soren. They are bound to a place and then feed on the souls of those unfortunate enough to wander or be sent within their influence. Whoever prisoned it here has also erased evidence of disappearance and death from the minds of everyone."

"How do we stop it?"

"With fire and a draiochta sword."

"Do we have one of those among us?" he asked.

"We'll see. It often takes a threat from some form of magic to awaken the blade," she said.

Great. We're all dead, he thought.

As each guard moved off of the stairs, the line snaked down. Thomas put his foot on the floor and a shriek exploded from the left. Everyone crouched and spun toward the sound, swords ready. Torchlight wavered in a cold draft.

"Move out of the way and let everyone else off the stairs," Lady Aeden commanded. A low moan shivered through the undercroft again.

Thomas felt a tightening in his brain. He stumbled forward into Lady Aeden, clutching at her tunic as he fell. "Lady", he gasped. "I feel something in my mind!"

His knees hit the floor as he dropped his knife and grabbed his head with his hands. He gasped in pain as he curled into a ball.

Aeden, face grim, slammed to the floor on her knees next to him, her left hand clamping to the top of his head. She held her right hand aloft. Suddenly a fiery sword gleamed brightly in her hand, lighting the undercroft corridor. The children screamed. Soldiers gasped and reflexively stepped back.

Thomas relaxed with a sigh as she projected a shield over his mind.

"Thank you, Lady. What *was* that?" he exclaimed.

"As I thought, Lord Thomas. It *is* a seleigh soren. The practice you've done shielding your mind kept it from taking you as you came down the stairs. Whoever bound it here probably gave it your mental scent to take you first," she murmured to him. "That takes a fair amount of power. We must find who set this trap."

The soldiers were backing slowly away from where Thomas lay and Lady Aeden still held her gleaming sword aloft. The children were huddled together in a tight group at the bottom of the stairs, Breanna openly weeping.

Lady Aeden slowly lowered her sword as she stood. Angry shrieks echoed through the corridors of the undercroft. The soldiers in the hallway whirled to face outwards and crouched, prepared for any attack.

Those still bunched on the stairs hurriedly descended and joined the group at the bottom. Lady Aeden extended a hand to Thomas, who grasped it and let her pull him to his feet.

"Do you feel anything now?" she asked.

"No. It just feels like there's an iron band around my head." He shuddered. He felt sick and very tired.

"That's your shield," she responded. "Try to loosen it a bit."

Thomas put his shaking hand on the side of his head, stilled his mind and grounded his ki, sending mental roots deep into the earth. As he did, the pressure eased until he was able to think again. "Ah," he sighed.

He was finally able to take note of what was happening around them. He picked up his knife from where he had dropped it.

The soldiers who had first descended the stairs formed a circle around them. They looked at Lady Aeden and her sword warily. Thomas snorted and shook his head. He thrust his knife into the sheath on his belt.

He'd thought that it would be a better weapon to use in the tight confines of the undercroft corridors.

He pulled his sword from its scabbard. As it cleared the hardened leather, light burst from the blade.

Lady Aeden grinned. "Yes!" she hissed.

The soldiers moved farther away from both of them.

Chapter 22

The draiochta sword flamed. Thomas turned his stunned face to the blade. Its light pulsed with the beat of his blood. It had never done anything like *this* before.

Lady Aeden regarded him and the sword soberly. "Lord Thomas, I'm very glad that you chose that sword. They often name themselves. Has it told you its name? Drop your shields. I'll protect you," she demanded urgently.

Oh good gods. Thomas was scared.

He slowly opened the shields he had erected to protect his mind. He felt the extra shielding that Lady Aeden provided.

"Hello?" he questioned hesitantly. *How do you talk to a sword?*

A rumbling wicked chuckle met his question. He jerked and almost dropped the blade.

A deep voice thrummed through every mind. Shouts and cries of fear filled the corridor.

I am glad to be taken up once again! It has been long and long. I thirst for battle.

Thomas started violently, wanting to drop the glowing sword. "What is that?" he exclaimed.

"Not what, Lord Thomas, but whom," said his teacher.

Hello, young whelp of the Arach's. I slumbered long, waited for this moment to come again. What are you called? The voice echoed again in all of their minds.

Thomas looked at Lady Aeden with eyes gone wide and all color drained from his face. The sword shook in his hand. A jolt of power up his arm jerked his eyes back to the sword.

I am Thomas, son of Thomas, son of John. Who might you be? He asked the question very politely.

I am a Draiochta Sword. I have ever fought against the power of the Demon host. I can feel them rising. Let us finish this evil that rests at the heart of Red Dragon's Keep. The sword spoke to him alone.

Thomas turned to Aeden. "He names himself a Draiochta Sword. He wants to finish the seleigh soren."

Thomas watched Lady Aeden's eyes widen. She gave a tiny gasp then sketched a slight bow to the sword. "You honor us with your presence," she murmured. Thomas looked at her with raised eyebrows. "Lady, did you know?"

"I suspected," she answered.

I am HellReaver, born of wizard power and Dragon fire, used by the Arachs since the line was born. I greet you Lord Thomas and Lady Aeden. Lady Aeden, it is good to greet you and OathKeeper once again.

Lady Aeden looked puzzled. Thomas shook his head. A shriek filled his ears. "We need to kill this thing."

It is a seleigh soren, HellReaver, bound here to take Lord Thomas by someone above, Lady Aeden exclaimed in Thomas's mind.

Let us be about it then, kill this Demon and finish the traitor who tried to kill you. The light of the sword damped down to a very dim glow.

Thomas straightened. He looked at the soldiers surrounding them and pointed to the left. "The seleigh soren is that way. Lady Aeden and I will take point. Owen, Cameron, Evan and Breanna, stay with Sergeant Padric. Be ready."

Cameron quavered a question, "Thomas, what *is* that?" pointing at the sword.

Thomas looked at Lady Aeden. "This is HellReaver. He is an ancient ally of our family," he said, turning to the group. "He will help us defeat the Demon held here to kill us." Eyes widened even further all around.

"And I hold OathKeeper, companion for many years," said Lady Aeden.

Thomas and Lady Aeden moved toward the front of the group.

The soldiers backed hastily to the sides of the corridor to let them pass. The Keep had two wells, one between the forecourt and stables, the other in the undercroft of the Tower close to the kitchens. He thought that's where the monster was imprisoned. Another shriek seemed to shake the walls. Swiftly they moved forward, all need for quiet or stealth gone.

The corridor ended at the well-room, the entry itself opening on the left hand side of the hall. Thomas and Aeden put their backs to the walls on either side of the entry as the others grouped a few feet away. Aeden and Thomas looked past the doorway into the room.

At least ten bodies covered the floor in various states of dismemberment. Thomas gagged. The smell was horrific, decaying meat and the iron tang of old blood.

In the center of the room a being from a nightmare stood enclosed by shimmering bars of light and power.

The seleigh soren was grey. It looked vaguely human, skin hanging in rotting, cadaverous folds from every joint. Hands with but three fingers reached toward the bars of light and the creature screamed as they made contact. A high domed head with slits for a nose sat directly on the things shoulders. Its eyes gleamed blood red in deep black eye sockets. Drool dripped from its mouth filled with sharp jagged teeth. It reached again toward them.

Sergeant Padric sighed. "My Lord, this 'seleigh soren' can't be a threat. She's beautiful."

Thomas's head whipped toward the soldier. "What?" he exclaimed.

Lady Aeden slashed her upraised hand across her body, wordlessly telling him to wait. "What do you see?" she demanded.

"I see a young woman weeping in the center of the room," Sergeant Padric said, tilting his head in inquiry. "What do you see?" he asked.

Thomas described the apparition of horror.

Padric blanched.

Thomas turned to Lady Aeden.

There is only one way to kill this Demon spawn,
HellReaver spoke in their minds. *It cannot be banished.*
You must break the bars of power and cleave the creature from
head to toe before it can escape. Both of you must set it afire.

Thomas gulped. He looked at the bodies destroyed by
this monster. His eyes narrowed as his jaw clenched.
These were people that he'd been charged with protecting. "Let's finish this."

They surged into the well-room. Lady Aeden slashed
her sword through the bars of power. She fell to one
knee as her power was sucked away then backlashed into her body.

The Demon leaped at Thomas as the spell containing
it shattered. Thomas lifted HellReaver and slashed
across the arms of the beast. It shrieked in agony. Green
fluid gushed from the gashes. He swung his sword back
across its body. As its blood splattered his tunic, the fabric began to smolder.

The Demon shrieked again. OathKeeper burst into
flame. Lady Aeden flowed to her feet and moved to
stand in front of the door, forbidding exit.

The soleigh soren flung itself, mouth agape, at
Thomas and tried to grasp him with its bleeding arms.
It lunged toward his throat.

Thomas swung HellReaver over his head and brought
it down on the creature with all the strength in his arms.
HellReaver flashed white and Thomas howled in battle
fury. The sword sliced through head and body as if it
was made of butter.

The two halves fell to either side as he staggered forward over it. He whirled with HellReaver held at guard,

ready to take on any threat. As he turned, clawed hands scrabbled toward his legs dragging the sundered body toward him. He swung HellReaver again and digits flew across the room.

Lady Aeden chanted a fire spell that ignited the scattered body of the monster.

Thomas added his fire spell to hers with a gesture of his hand.

Lady Aeden stood to his right, leaning on the tip of her sword. The backlash of released power had hit her hard.

The cleaved body of the seleigh soren began to smoke and bubble as the mage-fire began to consume it. The smell of smoke, death and decay filled the room and corridor beyond.

Suddenly exhausted, Thomas lowered HellReaver and moved to Aeden's side as the battle rage drained from his body. He laid the sword at his feet and stripped off his burned and pockmarked tunic, throwing it on the flames consuming the Demon.

"Let's go up. We'll leave this to burn itself out then send a crew to remove what's left." He picked up HellReaver.

Slowly they walked from the room and joined the others waiting in the corridor.

Thomas waved his hand toward the staircase.

"It's dead. We're safe for now."

Soldiers straightened in relief and sheathed their swords.

Owen, Breanna, Cameron and Evan sighed and sheathed their knives. "Wow. I can't believe that thing was down here and nobody knew," exclaimed Owen. Breanna stood as close to him as she could, shivering violently. He put his arm around her and started to rub her arm, trying to calm her down.

Cameron and Evan stood looking into the room, watching as the flames consumed the body. They looked at each other and then grinned. "That was excellent, Thomas! Lady Aeden, you were great!" they shouted together. Thomas just shook his head.

They all turned and, as the energy of fear and battle-readiness drained from their bodies, they trudged wearily back up the stairs.

Chapter 23

Thomas sat alone at one of the tables in the great hall, cleaning HellReaver with a soft rag soaked in oil. The fire burning in the hearth cracked and snapped as the great logs burned down to ash. Pleasant warmth enveloped his back.

He brought out his whetstone to sharpen the blade. The rhythmic rasp soothed him. This was a mindless task he had done so many times in the recent past that it left his mind free to wander.

HellReaver, why didn't we know you were here? How long have you been here? Why didn't my father choose you?

HellReaver responded. *Your father has not chosen a Sword of Light. He has always carried the sword of his house. The swords of houses are symbols of power and rank in the kingdom. This knowledge has been lost along with so much else during the time I have been quiescent.*

When your father returns, he must choose a Sword of Light. Recall the drawing you felt at your choosing? He will feel the same.

I have been waiting for you, young Thomas. Time to me is lost in dreaming of ages past. My last bearer was Laef Arach, over two centuries ago as you count time.

Your father will bear BattleSworn. Others will be taken up.

We of the Claiomh Solas, the Swords of Light, are awakened once again.

Thomas sat stunned, whetstone dangling limp from his hand. This was a sword out of legend.

By the gods, he thought, *we are doomed if I hold a Sword of Light!*

§ § §

The next day, Gregory found him at breakfast. Tired beyond measuring following the battle with the Soleigh Soren, Thomas ate, not tasting, food moving from trencher to mouth without thought.

Dawn light was barely breaking the horizon, heralding another icy fall day. He had dressed warmly in woolen trousers and doublet to keep the cold that permeated the Tower at bay. Soldiers, skullies, and freemen filled the tables arranged in rows in the body of the great hall, eating breakfast before the start of their labors.

More and more of the freemen and their families who looked to the Keep for protection were arriving each day, driven from their Steadings by the advancing Demon hordes. Shelters were set up against the walls of the Keep, both inside and out and at the edge of the village beyond the cattle pens. There would soon be no room left within the wall that protected both the Keep and the village.

"My Lord," Gregory's voice spoke with regret. Thomas blinked and came back to the present with a start.

"I must remind you that we hold those who have betrayed us ready for your judgment. I also believe that it is the better part of safety to have soldiers assigned to guard you. You are the heir and must be protected."

Thomas groaned and pushed himself back in his chair.

Gregory shook his head in sympathy. "I understand, my Lord. This isn't something that any of us is looking forward to."

"Is there anyone here who can question them?" Thomas asked.

"The captain of the guard may have the expertise." Gregory ran a hand through his already disordered hair and glanced down the tables. "Lance Corporal, go to the barracks and request that Captain Braden report here."

"Yes sir." the lance corporal jumped up and hurried out of the great hall.

"What of Lady Aeden. Do you think she might help?" asked Thomas.

"All we can do is ask her, Lord Thomas," Gregory said, shaking his head. "And here she is now." He smiled as Lady Aeden entered the room from the direction of the kitchen and storerooms. "I'll let four soldiers whom I trust know that they are to be your guards from now on."

Thomas closed his eyes and leaned his head against the back of his chair. He didn't want guards, but understood the need.

He really, really didn't want to ask Lady Aeden if she would question the traitors. He was afraid of her answer, either way.

Lady Aeden tipped her head in question as she walked toward them. "What is it?"

Once she stood at the table with them, Thomas asked, "My Lady, I don't want to ask this of you. I have to. Will you question the traitors with me and Captain Braden? I don't know the questions to ask."

Lady Aeden crossed her arms over her chest. She looked at the wall behind the table, her mind obviously focused far away.

"My Lady? Are you all right?"

Aeden came back from her thoughts. "All is well, Lord Thomas. I was remembering a questioning in my past. It wasn't pleasant." With a sigh, she agreed. "Yes, I'll help with questioning those who would endanger us all."

Thomas pushed himself out of his chair. "I don't understand why or how someone I have known all my life can be a traitor." He shook his head. "It makes no sense." Thomas pounded his right fist into his left hand over and over again. "How could she," he kept muttering.

"There is no reason for her to do this," he exclaimed, throwing his arms wide. "She had a home here, a good job and we all loved her."

Gregory looked at Thomas with sympathy. "I might have an answer for you, Lord Thomas. Jalyn was the headwoman after Lady Eirin, your grandmother, died. Your grandfather, Lord John, lost interest in everything after she was gone.

Jalyn took over and ran the daily life of the Keep with an iron hand until your father married Lady Jenni. Jalyn and Lady Jenni did not get along. Jalyn became the cook, which is quite a fall from her former position." Gregory shook his head. "She has carried this anger for fifteen years."

Lady Aeden reached out and clasped him by the arm. "People change. People let things eat at them until they are no longer the person that you knew. We will find the reasons that she would do this. Come. I must set the wards." She gave him a shake.

"Where should we conduct the questioning?" Thomas asked.

"Perhaps my office would do?" Gregory offered.

"Can you ward that space, Lady?" asked Thomas.

"Yes I can," she responded. "Have the guards bring the prisoners one at a time to the office."

"Yes, my Lady." Gregory turned to the sergeant in charge of Thomas's escort detail. "Please bring the traitor Jalyn to my office. Use four guards to escort her." The guard hurried away to the holding room.

Thomas, Gregory and Lady Aeden made their way to the seneschal's office.

As the trio turned the corner to Gregory's office, Captain Braden approached down the hallway from the kitchen. He saluted Thomas as he came to a stop in front of Gregory's door. "Lord Thomas. How may I be of service?" he asked.

"Captain Braden, we need to question the traitors who have betrayed us; find out what they have done and with whom they are in league," Thomas told him. "Lady Aeden has agreed to ward the room and help with the questioning."

Captain Braden nodded.

They walked through the door and moved to the windows, turning to look at her as Lady Aeden took her place in the center of the room, facing east. She bowed her head and closed her eyes, then opened them and raised her arms over her head so that her palms met, her arms forming a circle.

"I call the East, to the element of Air." She turned one quarter turn to the right and brought her arms down to her sides.

"I call the South, to the element of Fire." Another quarter turn to the right. She raised her arms and crossed them in front of her chest.

"I call the West, to the element of Water." She turned a final quarter turn to face north. She raised her arms to shoulder height.

"I call the North, to the element of Earth." Her arms swung down to her sides.

"I call the Spirit, the ruler of all." She thrust her arms skywards as if she were throwing a shower of magic into the air.

"Ward this space and keep all safe. As I will, so shall it be."

Thomas felt the surge of magic from each cardinal direction as the Lady called to them. He could feel pillars of power take form in each place.

A scream echoed in the hall outside of the door. "No, no, no! Don't take me in there! It's killing me! AHHH!"

Flanked by two guards, Jalyn, her hands chained in front of her and heavy chains on her ankles, was shoved into the room by the two guards behind her. She fell heavily to her knees on the floor in front of Aeden.

The four guards took up positions on either side of the door and directly across the hall from the room. Nothing was going to get in or out.

Jalyn moaned and rocked from side to side, her face contorted in pain. "No, no, no," she repeated again and again.

Captain Braden grabbed her arms and dragged her to her feet. "Shut up," he snapped sharply.

Jalyn's face was swollen from crying. She clasped her hands in supplication and fell to her knees again. "Please, kill me now. What He will do is worse than anything you can dream of."

"Who are you talking about," growled Captain Braden.

Her eyes suddenly glittered in triumph, her mouth twisted in hate. "The High Draiolc of the Ciardha Demon."

"What have you done?" gasped Thomas in shock.

Aeden, Gregory and Captain Braden erupted with questions and exclamations.

"What?" Aeden exclaimed.

"How could you," shouted Gregory.

Thomas grasped the pommel of his sword. As he did, HellReaver demanded *Draw me.*

Thomas pulled the Sword of Light from its scabbard. Light flared. Thomas laid the edge of the sword against Jalyn' neck.

"Speak, traitor, and tell us of your treachery." HellReaver's voice echoed in all of their minds.

Jalyn gagged and her back arched in terror as the sword spoke in her mind. She jerked away from the touch of the blade.

Thomas wondered distantly how someone so fat could move that quickly.

"What have you done?" Captain Braden's question grated out.

"Your grain is rotting, the flour is gone. Meat will spoil quickly now. The gates will fall. Soon the wells will be poisoned. You are all dead!" Jalyn shrieked. "Lord Mannan brings the horde to take this stronghold. We have made certain that you will fall." She laughed hysterically. Her face contorted into a mask of fear and hate. Her eyes gleamed maniacally.

She lunged toward HellReaver, intent on impaling herself on the sharp blade. Lady Aeden snapped her hand out and Jalyn froze.

"I've but one question for you, traitor." Thomas spoke slowly and evenly. "Why?"

"I should have been chatelaine of this Keep. You and yours are nothing." Her bitterness flowed like acid through her words. "Lord John should have chosen me for his wife after your grandmother died. Instead, he wasted away for *nothing!*" she shouted.

Stunned silence echoed in the room.

Lady Aeden applied pressure to the neck of the lump of quivering fat. Jalyn gagged. "What are you promised?"

"I will be the ruler of this Keep. You will be either dead or my slaves. I will beat each of you until you are bloody and broken, and then you die." Jalyn grunted a wicked laugh as Captain Braden kicked her.

"Who are your partners in this treason?" Captain Braden spoke through clenched teeth.

Lady Aeden squeezed her fingers together. Jalyn gagged again.

"Look to Hugo and the other stablemen. Look to the squires and the men-at-arms. Question everyone and you'll still not find them all."

Captain Braden turned to Thomas. "The sentence for treason is death, my Lord."

Thomas looked at Gregory. Gregory nodded. He looked at Aeden and Captain Braden. Both of them nodded.

He found his voice. "Take this offal and hang her. Make sure she is dead. Burn the body. Do it now."

Thomas felt as though he had been turned to stone. A sick feeling churned in his stomach.

"Guards," barked Captain Braden.

Two of the guards in the corridor entered the study and grabbed Jalyn by her manacles, jerking her to her feet. She screamed, ranted, and raved as they dragged her away down the corridor, throwing herself from side to side in an attempt to escape.

Thomas followed them into the hallway and stood watching, arms folded across his chest.

Her cries ceased abruptly as one of the guards backhanded her across the face, stunning her into silence.

"Captain Braden, bring in the next prisoner," Thomas snapped. He walked back into the room.

Chapter 24

The grounds of Red Dragon's Keep were huge. The inner wall surrounding the Dragon Tower stood three stories tall. Massive gates were thrown open, giving access to the tower.

The outer wall extended to the north and then west around the town before circling back and joining the inner wall surrounding the tower. Shops and houses, gardens and corrals, filled the space between the inner and outer walls of the Keep.

Hasty shelters had been built along the outer walls of the Keep itself to provide housing for the freeholders streaming in from the countryside. The villagers had opened their homes to those who had nowhere else to go.

Every speck of grain and food that could be brought to the Keep was rolling in on carts pulled by oxen or barrows pushed by farmers. Herds of cattle and sheep grazed on the increasingly scarce grass surrounding the Keep and town. The small river that meandered through the valley had provided enough water so far. The Dragon Tower itself had two wells inside its walls.

Marta and her family, as well as the members of the Steading who had survived the journey and the Demon attacks, trudged wearily toward the double gates in the wall surrounding Red Dragon's Keep and the village beyond. They joined other families and merchant trains making toward the dubious safety to be found within.

Guards checked each person, horse and wagon seeking to enter. *Do they think Demons are hiding in backpacks or wagons?* Marta mocked silently.

The line finally moved enough to get them through the gates and into the Keep proper. The group stopped and gawked at the massive tower with its Dragon spiraling up the east wall set in red stone.

"I've never seen anything the like," said Kevin, Marta's younger brother.

"Where do we stay?" asked ever practical Raina.

The Halorans followed the moving mass of people and came to the main thoroughfare passing through the village.

"I'll ask one of the soldiers what we should do," Faolan rumbled to Raina. Marta knew that he'd served in the King's Army with Duke Arach. He'd lived at Red Dragon's Keep until he'd been granted a Steading for his service and met and married Raina from the village near his land.

Stepping to the side of the road out of traffic, Haloran raised his voice to be heard by his remaining holders. "All of you have relatives here. If you need anything, find me and I'll see what I can do to help," he told them.

The men and women clustered around him, patting him on the back and shaking his hand, thanking him for bringing them this far. When they were done, they and their younglings moved off to find their kin.

A troop of cavalry trotted their horses down the busy street. At its head rode a tall young man on a blood-bay charger. Marta gasped. The cage of six chickens that she was carrying crashed to the paving stones that covered the street. The cage shattered and chickens flapped and cackled wildly across the street, startling the line of horses into shying and bucking.

Marta's face went white, and then red stained her cheeks in embarrassment. She had seen that rider in her dreaming for as long as she could remember. "Mother, who is that?" she choked out as she grabbed her mother's arm.

Raina looked at her blankly. "How should I know, Marta? I've never been to Red Dragon's Keep before."

The young man managed to bring his horse under control. He scowled at Marta and growled out, "What are you doing, woman? You could have caused injury or death here."

Marta dropped her head. "I'm sorry, sir. You startled me, that's all."

$$\S \S \S$$

Thomas looked more closely at the girl. She was tall and slim with golden skin. Her black hair was pulled back into a tail that fell to the middle of her back. Her clothing, though worn, was clean. He'd caught a glimpse of stormy green eyes before she had looked at the ground. He felt a quick jab to his heart. He frowned.

He looked at the rest of the group. His horse sidled nervously. "Have you just arrived at Red Dragon's Keep?" he asked. "Heddwyn, stop it." He jerked sharply on his mount's reins to stop his movement. The horse threw his head up, away from the bit. "Sorry," he said to the group of refugees. "I'm Thomas. Can I help you?"

Faolan pushed between his sons and stood next to Marta. "Hello, Thomas. Sorry for my daughter's clumsiness. I served with Duke Arach during the war. We've come because the Demons have attacked our Steading. Would you know where we can stay?"

Thomas gazed thoughtfully at the five. *This is perfect. They may have the information that we need.* "I'm Lord Arach's son. I'd like to talk to you about what happened. Go to the Keep and ask for Gregory. Tell him I want you to have quarters in the guest wing. We'll talk as soon as I'm back from patrol. That's about four candlemarks."

"Thank you, Lord Thomas. We'll be there," Faolan choked out as he gave a slight bow.

Thomas reined Heddwyn around as the column reformed. He looked at all of them. "I'm glad you've come safe to us. We'll need every hand to beat back the Dark."

$$\S\,\S\,\S$$

Faolan and his family walked slowly toward the wall that enclosed the square tower rising in the center of Red Dragon's Keep. They approached the gate that opened into the inner Keep grounds surrounding the stronghold. The private stationed at the gate stepped into its opening. "Halt," he ordered. "State your business."

"Lord Thomas told us to come and speak to Gregory about staying here," Faolan told the very young soldier. The young man didn't recognize him.

The private eyed the group and then called out to the sergeant in charge. "Sergeant, this fellow says that Lord Thomas told them to come here for housing."

The sergeant stepped out of the guard house and looked the family members over. He didn't recognize Faolan, either. Dust rose from the shuffle of feet along the road through the Keep, tickling Marta's nose and throat. She sneezed, and sneezed again.

"Send a man to get Gregory," he ordered the private. "You wait here," he ordered the group.

Gregory stomped toward the family. As he drew nearer, he recognized Faolan and broke into a jog. As he reached them, he clasped Faolan's outstretched hand and grasped his other arm with his left hand. "Faolan! It's good to see you again. What brings you to the Keep?" he exclaimed.

"We had to come, Gregory. The Demons attacked and drove us out. If we hadn't left when we did, we'd all be dead," he told his old friend with grim resignation.

Gregory slowly let go of his hand. "I'm sorry, Faolan. How many did you lose?" he asked quietly.

"Over half of my people," Faolan told him.

Gregory shook his head in dismay. "And Rand, your father?"

"Killed two days ago in a Demon attack," he replied.

Gregory took a deep breath. Then another. "He was a good man," he said simply.

Shaking off the bad news, Gregory looked at Faolan's family. "Lord Thomas told you to come here? I expect he'll want to talk to you about your journey, see if anything bears on what we need to do. Come on. I'll have guest quarters readied for you." He turned and led them across the forecourt, up the stairs and into the tower.

§ § §

The Halorans stood in the center of the suite of rooms that Gregory had assigned them. Raina, the boys and Marta craned their necks, looking at the tapestries on the walls, the low table and chairs in the center of the room and the long tables set between four doors, two on one side of the main room and two on the other. Faolan watched in amusement. He'd been here before and recognized the suite.

"Raina, you and I will stay in this room." He waved toward the door on the left closest to the suite entrance. "Boy's, you take that one." He pointed at the room next to his and Raina's. "Marta, take that one." He pointed to the door opposite her brothers'. "Put your things away and meet back here when you're done," he told them. He and Raina walked through the door into their room. Jaiman and Kevin looked at each other, grinned, and hurried through their door.

Marta looked around the room and shrugged in annoyance. She'd wanted the room next to her parents.

She cautiously entered her room. It held a bed, a fireplace, a wardrobe and a commode with a basin and pitcher on top. The bed had four posts that rose almost to the ceiling connected with rods from which depended thick curtains pulled back to reveal a feather filled mattress covered with wool blankets and quilts. Shutters were folded back on either side of the window that looked out on the stables and a training yard. A trunk sat at the foot of the bed. She swung her pack onto the trunk and then sat down next to the pack. Her shoulders slumped. All she wanted to do was sleep.

Raina knocked on the door frame and walked through the doorway. She scanned the room curiously, and then walked over to Marta. "A bit much for us, isn't it?" she asked quietly.

"I don't know what to do, Mama. Where should I put my things? What should I do?" she almost wailed.

Raina pulled her into a hug. "It will be all right, I promise. You'll get used to all of this soon enough." She let go of Marta and walked over to the bed, sitting gingerly on the edge. "Come here," she patted the mattress next to her. "I need to ask you about what happened with the chickens. Why did you ask me who he was when you saw Lord Thomas?"

Marta walked to the bedside and reluctantly sat on the mattress. She didn't want to get it dirty. It gave pleasantly under her weight. She avoided looking at her mother, gazing out of the window instead. "I've never told you about my dreams. I didn't want to worry you. I've been dreaming about him for as long as I can remember, Mama. They've been dreams about him growing up, playing with his brother and sister," she said. "Fighting Demons," she added. "It feels like he's always there, in the back of my mind."

Raina's eyes widened as her daughter talked. There had been some in her family who dreamed true. She'd never thought one of her children might have that gift, or curse, as the case might be. "Are they the same Demons that we've been fighting?" she asked.

"Yes. I was afraid to tell you. I thought that my dreaming might be why they were attacking us," she whispered.

"Oh, Marta, no. That's not what dreaming true does. It shows possible futures. At least that's what I've been told. It's a fearsome gift. I wish you had told me. My mother told me that it helps if you write the dreams down. She could dream true, too." She sighed. "I'll get you some paper or a book to write in." She stood up and patted Marta on the shoulder. "Let me know if you have any more Dreams," she said, capitalizing the word with her voice. "Come now. Let's go down for mid-meal."

$$\S\,\S\,\S$$

Thomas rode back to the Keep with his patrol as the sun began to set. He tossed Heddwyn's reins to a groom as he dismounted. "Rub him down well and let him out with the others. He's done a good day's work." He gave the horse an affectionate slap on the neck as he turned to walk toward the kitchen entrance to the Tower.

His patrol had seen plenty of destruction of freeholds and Steadings as they rode, but no Demons. No one could answer the question of where they were hiding during the day. Thomas took the stairs two at a time into the kitchen.

He grabbed a meat pie as he passed the table where they were cooling for the evening meal. "Good afternoon, Mistress Clara. These are great." he told the temporary head cook as he took a bite.

"Good afternoon, Thomas, I mean Lord Thomas," she responded, blushing. They had grown up together and knew each other well. Clara had taken over the kitchen when Jalyn had been - removed. Things moved just as smoothly under her direction as they ever had under Jalyn and everyone was a lot more cheerful.

"When will the new cook be chosen?" she asked hesitantly. "I'd really like to return to my duties as the pastry cook."

"I don't know," Thomas said. "I'll check with Gregory and tell him you asked."

"Thank you, my Lord."

He strode through the room and into the great hall corridor. Gregory was hurrying down the hall and called to him. Thomas turned and noted the concerned look on his face. "What's wrong?" he asked.

"Faolan Haloran and his family arrived. I've put them in the guest wing as you requested. You do realize that he was the Master Sergeant in charge of troops during the war, don't you?"

"No, he only said that he'd served with Father in the war," Thomas gulped. He was very glad that he'd been polite and sent them to the Tower. "I'd like to meet with him as soon as possible, if you think it wise."

"Oh, yes," said Gregory. "They've been running and fighting for weeks and might have some answers to where the Demons go during the day and what may be controlling them. I'd suggest Lady Aeden and Captain Braden attend. The Library is probably the best place."

"Fine. Let's meet there in a candlemark. I need a bath and change of clothes. Have you seen Owen and Breanna? Oh, and Cameron and Evan. They should hear this as well."

"I'll send for them now," Gregory said.

A candlemark later, Thomas climbed the stairs to the Library.

He could hear conversation as he approached. The Halorans were deep in discussion with Gregory, Lady Aeden and Thomas's brother, sister and cousins about the running fight that had brought them to Red Dragon's Keep. As he entered, they all stood.

Embarrassed, Thomas waved them back to their seats at the large table that filled the center of the room. He walked to the chair at the head of the table and sat.

"Good evening, everyone. What have I missed?"

Faolan stood and introduced his family. "My Lord, this is Raina, my wife. These are my sons, Jaiman and Kevin, and you met Marta this morning," he concluded with a half grin.

Thomas nodded to each as they were named. His eyes lingered on Marta until he jerked them away.

She refused to look at him.

Faolan's attitude changed and he shook his head wearily. "My Lord, we've been on the run for almost three weeks. We could only go as fast as the elderlies among us. It seemed like forever. We lost more than half of the holders who looked to us for protection. The Demons attacked almost every single day; at dusk, during the night and in the early morning."

He scrubbed at his face. "The only way to kill them is to let them get close and run them through or shoot flaming arrows at them. Spears work but swords are chancy. They run right up the blade and kill even while they are dying."

Raina chimed in, "They won't cross running water. It almost seems to burn them if they get into it. They kill and eat everything."

"Do you have any idea who or what is commanding them?" Lady Aeden asked.

"Twice we saw some kind of winged creatures perching in the trees in the gloom as they attacked," said Faolan. "Marta was the one who caught that during one of their raids. We kept watch during the next one and didn't see anything. At the end of the last attack right before we reached Red Dragon's Keep, Kevin saw it again."

Thomas turned toward the girl who sat shyly behind her parents, trying to be invisible. "Marta, can you tell us what you saw?"

She squirmed in her chair when she was singled out. "My Lord, Lady, it was very dark and I couldn't see well. My night-vision was gone and the firelight hid most of the surroundings even though the fire was very large. The creature had great wings that were folded at its sides. The tips of its wings rose above its head by half again its size. It looked like it had large pointed ears. Its arms were crossed over its chest. I couldn't tell if it was clothed. After the second attack failed, the creature flew away to the south and west."

Thomas looked at her steadily for what seemed like a very long time, thinking about what she had said. "Has anyone heard or read of anything like she describes?" He put his elbow on the table and rested his chin in his hand.

Lady Aeden cleared her throat. "I may have caught some gossip in the market about a flying creature cloaked in darkness guiding the Demons. It sounded like one of the tales told to children to make them behave."

"So here is what we know," Thomas said. "The Demons don't attack during the day, probably because they can't see. Maybe the light hurts their eyes. They won't cross running water. They burn. They can be killed, albeit better not in close combat. There is some kind of creature controlling them or at least directing them, maybe some kind of Smachtmaistir, a Demon controller. Does that about sum it up?"

Everyone thought for a moment, considering the information. Breanna added, "There are people working with them and they have a High Draiolc, a human sorcerer, working with them."

"You're right, Breanna," Thomas said. "There are spies and collaborators here and probably throughout the kingdom. I wonder what they hope to gain." He shook his head in frustration. "How do we use this information? What can we do to draw the Demons together and then defeat them? We need to learn the best way to kill them."

"What about an ambush?" both Owen and Cameron said at the same time. "Jinx," said Owen. "Don't talk until someone says your name," he ordered, pointing at Cameron. Cameron scowled.

"If we could get some of the Demons together right before the sun comes up or right after it goes down, maybe we can set them on fire or shoot them, see what works best," Owen suggested. "Cameron, you can talk now," he finished. Cameron stuck his tongue out at Owen.

"Hmm." Thomas considered. "Gregory, what do you think?"

Gregory frowned. "Perhaps we should start small. Take a troop of soldiers and freeholders and travel a week away from the Keep. Set up camp and be prepared for anything. Send out scouts to draw them in. That might work. At least you'll get in some practice killing them."

"How soon do you think we can set this up? If Jalyn wasn't lying and a host of Demons is on its way, maybe we should wait until they attack." Thomas stood and moved to the window behind his chair.

Do not wait, counseled HellReaver. *You must find out what works best to kill the beasts in large numbers. In the past, the Demons worked in small groups to harry and harass Steadings, travelers and patrols. A leader only emerged when the numbers of Demons became large enough that they could call it forth.*

"HellReaver suggests that we not wait. He says that we need to find out how the Demons fight. I think he's right," Thomas told the group.

The Halorans looked at each other in confusion.

"My Lord, who is HellReaver?" asked Faolan.

Thomas reached for his scabbard and drew his sword. HellReaver flamed with magelight.

The Halorans sat frozen in astonishment.

"This is HellReaver. He is a Sword of Light."

Greetings and well met, Faolan. You and yours are welcome indeed. HellReaver spoke to everyone.

Raina reached out and gripped Faolan's arm with fingers like steel.

"Well met, HellReaver," Faolan faltered with a small nod to the sword, patting Raina's hand.

"I agree, Lord Thomas," said Gregory with a chuckle.

Captain Braden echoed him, "We should try a small sortie."

"Very well. Captain Braden, pick thirty men and thirty freeholders," Thomas ordered. "We need enough able bodies here to guard the Keep. I'd like to leave first thing in the morning, two days from now. I think supplies for two weeks should be enough."

"Yes sir," Captain Braden said, as he saluted and left the room.

"Thomas, what do you want us to do?" asked Owen. "Should I go with you?"

"Not this time, Owen. If something happens to me, you're next in line as Father's heir. I think it would be better if you stayed here with Cameron, Evan, and Breanna and helped with setting up defenses for the Keep."

Breanna's lower lip trembled and tears filled her eyes.

"Nothing's going to happen to me, Breanna. It's just better to anticipate things and take steps to fix any problems before they happen," Thomas told his sister.

"I know, Thomas. I just wish it could be like it was before," she exclaimed.

"We all do, Breanna. Wishing won't fix it, so we need to make it happen. It will get better, I promise." Thomas walked around the table and gave Breanna a hug.

She reached up and clung to him for a moment.

"My Lord, I'd like to come, with my two sons," Faolan volunteered. "There are half a dozen freeholders who are women who would make good leaders here at the Keep. Raina and Marta are well versed in this type of warfare," he suggested.

"Thanks for volunteering, Faolan," said Thomas. "Would you take charge of the men under Captain Braden? I know you were the Master Sergeant in charge during the last war. Would you serve so again?"

"Yes I would, My Lord. Kevin, Jaiman, let's go and get ready." Faolan stood and touched his right fist to left shoulder. He and the boys stood up from the table and left the room.

"Lady Aeden, will you come with us?"

Aeden looked at Thomas and gave him a crooked smile. "Nothing could keep me away," she said. "Come,

Raina and Marta. Let's get you set up with the other freeholders staying here. Owen, Cameron, Evan, Breanna, come with us to help set defenses. My Lord, we'll see you at dinner." She saluted as well and herded everyone out of the Library.

Thomas turned and gazed pensively out of the east window, the same direction that his parents had taken to support the King. He felt as if he had shouldered one of the stones that made up Red Dragon's Keep. *What if I'm doing the wrong thing and throwing away lives that will be needed here?*

You are not, HellReaver spoke. *This step must be taken to ascertain the strength and tactics of the Ciardha Demon. Best do it now in a small way and win, than later when there are hordes and you lose. Do not forget I am with you, as is Lady Aeden.*

Thank you, HellReaver. I've not forgotten.

You must allow Lord Owen to choose his sword, as well as Cameron and Evan. They must start training immediately. Tonight is a good night for such a choice.

Thomas was startled at HellReaver's advice. *Don't you think they're too young?*

No. They're ready.

All right. Thomas left the Library for the great hall, shaking his head in wonder.

Chapter 25

"Owen, Cameron, Evan. HellReaver told me that you should choose your swords tonight. Lady Aeden, would you come with us?" Thomas asked after dinner.

Lady Aeden's left eyebrow rose in surprise. She glanced at the sword sheathed at Thomas's side. "Tonight?" she asked.

It is the night of the new moon, a fitting time for new beginnings, HellReaver replied.

"Ah," she responded. "I'd not paid attention. So it would."

The boys' eyes were huge.

"Come on. Let's get this done," said Thomas.

The boys, Thomas and Aeden rose from their tables and made their way through the tower, out across the receiving area behind the kitchen to the salle.

Night had fallen and the air was crisp and cold. Clouds crowded and darkened the western horizon, promising a storm by morning. They walked through the salle and into the hall that led to the armory.

The armory doors stood unguarded and locked. Lady Aeden frowned. "Lord Thomas?"

With a gesture, Thomas sent his magelight over the group.

Lady Aeden opened her left hand and magelight glowed within. "Isn't there supposed to be a guard?" she asked.

"Yes, there is," Thomas responded.

Shadows shrouded the ends of the hallway. Something didn't feel right.

"Get behind me," he whispered to the others. Darkness rustled and scraped to the right.

Thomas drew HellReaver from his scabbard. The sword flamed. Lady Aeden raised her hand and OathKeeper flared into being. Sword light threw the corridor into sharp relief.

Crouched in the corner was indeed a terrifying creature. Scales covered a grey and black form that stretched up and up until the tips of its folded wings nearly touched the ceiling. Blood red eyes gleamed at them. Claws at the end of impossibly long fingers reached out as if to rake them over bodies. A ridged muzzle filled with triangular teeth opened wide as a husky laugh filled the corridor.

"You have come to ME," it rasped. "How delightfully ironic. I do not have to invade the Tower itself!" Thunder boomed in the corridor as the monster spread its wings and slammed them down, racing toward the group.

They surged back against the wall and ducked with cries of fear. Thomas raised HellReaver with a shout and swung the sword at shoulder height. The blade bit deeply into the creature's shoulder and wing. Lady Aeden thrust OathKeeper into the creature's chest. Its' shriek spiraled higher and higher until the sound abruptly cut off and the creature disappeared.

"Ah, gods! What was that and where did it go?" gasped Thomas as he staggered against the wall.

"I don't know," Lady Aeden panted, hands on her knees. "I feel the lure of portal magic here in the corner. I'd lay odds that this is one of the betrayals that Jalyn worked in the Keep. Where there is one there will be more. We'll have to do a sweep of the entire Keep and neutralize every one of them."

She straightened and moved to the end of the hallway. "Yes. Here is the portal rune."

Everyone hurried to cluster behind her. Carved on the bottom stone of the corridor wall was a complicated rune that looked like a tree, arrows and a mountain enclosed in a star.

Aeden held her magelight close to the wall above the rune. She spoke three words. "Scrios seoathru doras."

A burst of bilious green light flashed from the rune as it disappeared, and stinking smoke filled the end of the corridor. The boys started coughing and backed away. Aeden turned her head and waved her hand in front of her face, her nose crinkling in disgust.

Turning toward the armory doors, she shooed the boys away from the disintegrated magic.

"Lord Thomas, please open the doors. Only one of your blood has that power once they are locked and guards are gone."

Thomas walked to the doors and laid his hand on the lock. It clicked open. Thomas just shook his head and pushed the doors open, waving his magelight into the room.

Owen, Cameron and Evan entered uncertainly, crowding behind Aeden as if for protection.

They stopped just inside the doors. Eyes darted along the line of weapons, and then turned in worry to Thomas and Aeden.

"It's all right," Thomas told them. "I know it's hard, but you need to calm down and think about something soothing, like maybe sleeping in the sun."

Lady Aeden put her hand on Owen's shoulder. "Remember what Thomas told you about choosing HellReaver? You must do the same thing. Calm. Listen to your gut and follow your heart."

§ § §

Owen looked apprehensively along the walls filled with weapons. He began his walk with tentative steps. He felt a drawing toward the right, so moved in that direction. He saw a short sword that fascinated him. As he walked toward it he was filled with certainty. This was his. He reached out and took the weapon in hand. Power flared through his body.

Welcome Owen. I am HeartStriker. We will do well together.

A smile of joy lit Owen's face. "He says his name is HeartStriker!"

§ § §

Cameron looked at Lady Aeden. She gave him a solemn nod. He moved to the left, letting his heart lead. An ornate saber caught his eye and he moved unerringly to take it by its grip.

Cameron, I greet you gladly. Well met. I am called Ghost-Walker.

Cameron turned to Lady Aeden. "GhostWalker."

A primal shiver visibly shook her body.

$ $ $

Evan was bouncing lightly on his toes. "My turn?" he asked her. She nodded and smiled.

Evan already knew which sword was his. He walked straight down the right side of the room to the back wall and took a sword that was very plain with a black leather wrapped grip and basket guard. Unlike the other blades, this one was black but appeared to shimmer in the magelight.

I am ShadowSworn, Evan. We belong together.

"He is ShadowSworn," Evan said.

$ $ $

Lady Aeden looked at the eager young faces before her. She marveled that so many of the Claiomh Solas – the Swords of Light – were gathered here in this place. Almost as if someone had known what was coming and prepared for it.

"Come. Let's return to the Dragon Tower and get to know your blades," she said. "Thomas, tomorrow we must search the Keep for runes and signs of magic. An early start will still let you leave in two days."

Chapter 26

Thomas groaned as he pulled himself out of bed. He'd been up very late, searching the Keep from top to bottom for magical sabotage.

He, Lady Aeden, and, surprisingly, Breanna and Marta, had found eleven more portal runes from the highest room in the tower to one of the storage rooms in the lowest level. There had even been two in the stables. All of the runes carried the stink of Jalyn's treachery and the tang of some greater magic. Those portals would have allowed Demons to invade the Keep before anyone was aware they were there. Breanna had found over half of them.

Thomas pulled on his travel clothes that he'd had laid out last night. The threatening storm had not materialized, thank goodness. It was going to be hard enough traveling in the cold without a fresh layer of snow to impede them. His travel bags had been packed and were ready to be loaded on the back of his saddle.

You should have Breanna choose a weapon. She will be here and is sensitive to magic. She could be taken easily without her own protection, HellReaver informed him.

Thomas straightened in outrage. *My sister? Choose a weapon? What?*

Is Lady Aeden less of a threat because she is a woman? HellReaver chuckled and answered his own question. *Of course not. Take Breanna this morning to choose her weapon before you leave.*

Thomas threw his arms in the air and acquiesced as he moved to the bowl of warmed water that his chamberlain had left on the commode. *Fine. I'll take her after breakfast. Oh, she's going to love this. Is there going to be anyone left to teach her how to use it?*

Silence greeted his question.

Marta, Haloran's daughter, has been trained, the sword slowly responded. *If she agrees, she can continue training Owen, Cameron, and Evan, as well.*

I'll ask her to come with us when Breanna chooses, Thomas answered with brusque curtness. He was upset that his little sister needed to be armed to protect herself from danger. That was his job and he felt that he'd failed in his responsibility.

Better she have the skills and not need them, than need them and not have them.

Agreed, Thomas responded. He grabbed up his saddlebags and left for breakfast.

$ $ $

Thomas found Gregory walking to the great hall for his own breakfast.

"Gregory, would you please send for Marta Haloran? I'd like to ask her to step in and take over weapons training for my family. Faolan said that she'd been trained and there is no one else."

"I'll send for her at once, my Lord." Gregory looked at Thomas out of the corner of his eye. "Is something wrong, my Lord? You sound upset."

Thomas stopped abruptly. Gregory swung around to face him.

"HellReaver suggested that Breanna needs a weapon. *That's* why I'm angry. She shouldn't have to *do* this."

"I understand, Thomas. War changes everything. Better to face reality than live in a fantasy and regret it."

"I know," Thomas said glumly and started walking again. It had all been a game to him before Jalyn, before his parents had been taken. He'd give anything to go back to those days.

They entered the great hall together and Gregory moved to the end of the room to send a skully for Marta.

The enticing odors of bacon, sausage and eggs pulled Thomas to the long table set along the kitchen wall of the room. He filled his trencher and walked to his seat at the high table.

Captain Braden entered the room and walked to the table. "My Lord, the men are ready whenever you are. Roads are clear, according to the scouts I sent out early this morning."

"Thank you, Captain. It's going to be at least a candlemark. I've some family business that I need to take care of."

"Yes sir. I'll tell the troops to stand easy but hold themselves ready." He saluted and left.

"Boys, I need to talk to you after breakfast. There's one more thing that needs to be taken care of before I leave."

Owen, Cameron, and Evan looked at him alertly. He could tell they knew something was up. They'd each belted on their new swords. Breanna just kept staring glumly at her trencher.

Thomas hurriedly finished his meal and stood up. "We all need to go to the armory. Including you, Breanna." He gave her a crooked smile as she raised her head and looked at him, a question in her eyes.

"Come on, let's go." Before he could leave the table, Marta entered through the forecourt door. She was dressed in a long woolen plaid dress in muted blues and greens, a warm cloak and sturdy boots. Her hair was bound in a braid that fell down her back.

"Ah...Marta. Would you please come with us to the armory? We're just on our way there now."

"I'd be happy to, my Lord," Marta answered, keeping her eyes on the floor.

She joined the group as they left the great hall through the kitchen and walked across the receiving area, through the salle and down the hallway to the armory. "Morning, Marta," said Owen. Cameron and Evan grinned at her.

"I heard what happened here night before last. Were you able to find all of the portals?" she asked.

"Not sure, but I hope so. HellReaver thinks so."

Marta looked warily at the sword in its scabbard hanging at his hip, eyes wide and body tense.

No need to fear me, girl. There are much more danger-ous things about.

The sword spoke tartly in all of their minds. The boys giggled, Thomas's face turned red with embarrassment, and Breanna just rolled her eyes.

And there's no need for your skepticism, Breanna.

Breanna gave a little skip and bowed to the sword. "Sorry, HellReaver," she said insincerely.

"Your pardon please, HellReaver. I meant no disrespect." Marta blushed with embarrassment.

Two guards snapped to attention as Thomas and the group approached the armory doors.

"Good morning, Corporals. We're here to choose another blade. Please open the doors."

The soldiers reached for the door handles and pulled them wide.

The sound of hurried footsteps approaching caused Thomas to crouch and swing around to face back the way they'd come, left hand on scabbard, right on HellReaver's grip, ready to draw. He straightened and released his grip as Lady Aeden stepped into the hall from the salle.

"Lord Thomas." She nodded at him. "Boys, Breanna." She grinned at all of them. "Welcome, Marta. Lord Thomas, I'd like to help if I may. Gregory told me about HellReaver's advice."

"I'm sorry, Lady Aeden. I'd have sent for you if I'd thought about it. HellReaver strongly suggested this morning that Breanna choose a weapon before we leave. Knocked everything else out of my mind."

Breanna's mouth fell open. "W...w...what?" she stammered. "Me?" she squeaked in astonishment.

"Yes, you. He's right. You need to be able to protect yourself if things go badly. Marta, your father said you'd had weapons training. Would you be willing to continue the training of these idle layabouts while we're gone?" he asked, waving his hand at his siblings and cousins as he grinned.

Lady Aeden looked at Marta. Slowly, she nodded. "That's an excellent idea, Lord Thomas. Marta, I join my request to his. They must continue training."

Marta stared at them, clearly dumbfounded, and hesitated. "Lady, Lord, yes, I've had training. I'm not sure that I've *enough* training. Is there no one else?

Both Thomas and Aeden shook their heads. "Everyone else is detailed to guard duty or patrolling," Thomas told her.

"All right," she conceded. "I'll do it. What I don't know, you all can teach me." She smiled at the boys and Breanna.

"Okay. Time to choose," Thomas said firmly.

They walked into the armory. A flash of white light illuminated the surroundings. Everyone flinched back. Two swords glowed with ethereal fire. Lady Aeden gasped. Marta moved left and Breanna moved right, as if drawn by an irresistible force. They each grasped their swords and raised them high, eerie flames blazing brightly.

"SunWalker," shouted Breanna.

"HellScream," gasped Marta.

The others looked on, frozen in shock.

"Oh my," whispered Lady Aeden.

Chapter 27

Thomas swung into his saddle and controlled Heddwyn's eager cavorting. "Captain Braden, you have the column," he barked. He wheeled Heddwyn around to the Tower steps and leaned down to clasp Owen's hand, then Breanna's, Cameron's and Evan's in turn. "Be safe. I'll send couriers with news." Reining his horse around, he signaled the tall blood-bay charger into a canter and took his place beside Captain Braden at the head of the column.

Tack jingled and wheels thundered as the column moved through the gates and onto the road that led toward Great Falls and Cathair Ri, the same road his parents had taken months ago. Thomas, Gregory and Captain Braden had chosen a waypoint five days toward Great Falls at the confluence of the Caladen and Banuisk rivers where they became the Samphir with its many tributaries. They'd set up the ambush there to hopefully draw the Demons.

§ § §

"Breanna, watch that drop at the end of your swing. Your target will come in over the top of your sword and stab you," Marta shouted. "Owen, up! Make sure that you swing up at the end of the cross-over. You must keep the rhythm or a thrust will get through."

Breanna, Owen, Cameron and Evan had been practicing with Marta twice a day for a week, trying to accomplish as quickly as possible what would normally take two or three months to master. They were all exhausted but worked doggedly to learn the battle skills they would need to fight the Demons they all knew were coming.

"Everyone take a break. We'll meet again after mid-meal." Marta dismissed her charges and followed them with weary steps into the Keep. Food had been set out on the head table for her little band.

Mid-meal had been over for a candlemark for everyone else. Each of them slumped down onto their chairs. They quickly drained the mugs of water that sat at each place. Each of them forked cold meats and vegetables from platters in the middle of the table on to their plates.

Marta was fourteen and the youngest of the Halorans. She took stock of each one of these children who had grown into the younger brothers and sisters that she'd always wanted. All of them needed more than a break for mid-meal, including herself. She decided to free everyone for the afternoon.

"All of you, I think we should take the afternoon off. Make sure your blades are cleaned and sharpened and then go do what you want." She smiled. "I'm going to take a nap."

The cousins looked at each other and grinned. Cameron said "Oh yeah. That's a good idea. I'm going to sleep, too." The others nodded in agreement.

Owen was the first finished, cleared his place and moved to the fireplace to clean HeartStriker. Cameron and Evan soon followed, with GhostWalker and ShadowSworn.

Breanna continued to sit at the table, drooping tiredly.

"Come on, Breanna. I'll help you clean SunWalker," Marta said quietly. "I need to take care of HellScream."

"Thanks Marta. I really need it," Breanna whispered. "My hands hurt a lot." She pushed back her chair and cleared her place, then followed Marta to the hearth.

Tomorrow, the Swords of Light will help you set your muscle memory. SunWalker spoke into all of their minds. *When that is done, each of you will not need to think of every step you take when fighting. We will strengthen your bodies so that you do not tire so easily. We have waited this long so that you would at least have the basics down. You all have done well. Marta, you are an excellent teacher.*

Eyes opened wide as the children listened to proof that somehow the swords they carried were alive and knew what was going on.

Owen spoke what they all were thinking. "Can you help us during the battle?"

Yes, we can, and we will. Each of you holds within yourself the seeds of greatness. We will help you nurture those seeds until you and they have matured.

"Do you know what kind of Demons we will face?" Cameron questioned in the silence that followed.

I only know those we fought in the far past. We will learn together and defeat each one. Do not fear.

"Thank you SunWalker, all of you swords. We are fortunate that you are here. Boys, Breanna, let's get this done and then take our time off," said Marta.

§ § §

Five days out from the Keep, Thomas shifted in his saddle, easing the cramping in his left calf. Heddwyn had finally settled down half a day after their departure. Even now, the warhorse watched the road vigilantly. Captain Braden moved up to ride beside Lady Aeden and him.

"My Lord, I think it's time for a break. The men and horses need it and we need lunch."

You need one, too. You won't be able to command anyone if you are too stiff to move. HellReaver spoke tartly in his mind.

"I agree, Captain. I definitely need a break. Let's call a halt," Thomas ordered.

Captain Braden reined his horse to the side and raised his fist in the signal to halt. He kicked his horse into a gallop towards the tail end of the column. Sergeants passed the command down the line of cavalry, foot troops and baggage wagons. The riders turned their horses onto the side of the road. They dismounted, loosened girths and removed bridles so the horses could graze on the sparse winter vegetation. Foot troops squatted where they stopped and pulled food from packs.

The weather was cold, but no snow covered the ground here. Thomas and Aeden dismounted, leading their horses to the side of the road next to the trees. They left the halter ropes that the horses wore under their bridles trailing on the ground. Thomas pulled jerky and journey bread from his saddle bag.

"Sergeant," he called. "Please have Master Sergeant Haloran report to me when he has a moment. Oh, and send Captain Braden back when you see him."

"Yes sir." The sergeant moved away.

Thomas and Aeden leaned against the trunks of the trees growing almost on the edge of the road. The ground was too cold and wet to sit on. They rested in companionable silence while each worked on chewing the tough jerky.

"What do you think of Marta?" Aeden asked him.

Thomas kept his eyes on the forest that started just beyond the verge. Between getting on the road and wondering if he'd be alive tomorrow, he'd thought about nothing else but her.

"I think she's a good fighter. I watched while you sparred with her. After that demonstration, I think she'll teach them what they need to know."

"She's well qualified," Aeden admitted.

"What do you think of her, my Lady?"

Aeden gazed down the road. "I think she's been through a lot in the last months. For all of that, she seems very grounded and steady. HellScream chose her." She shook her head. "Heroes rise when need calls. That's been said for centuries."

Thomas felt the drum of hoof-beats through the soles of his feet. He pushed himself away from the tree trunk and shaded his eyes with his hand. One of the point scouts came galloping toward them down the road. Clods of mud flew behind him. He pulled his horse to a stop next to Thomas and Aeden.

"Lord, Lady!" he exclaimed, panting with exertion. "A host of Demons approach through the forest from the south." He jumped from his horse, taking his weight from its back. "Half a day until they reach the convergence." Horse and rider hung their heads and panted for breath, the rider with hands on his knees.

Thomas moved to Aeden's side. "They're not supposed to move during the day," Thomas exclaimed. "Why are they moving now?"

"I don't know, Lord Thomas," Aeden replied. "Maybe their Smachtmaistirs are driving them to us despite the time of day."

Master Sergeant Haloran and Captain Braden led their horses toward the group.

"Captain, Sergeant. The scout says the Demons are moving toward the road during the day!" Thomas's heart raced. His breathing quickened and his hands and feet went numb. He trembled. Their strategy was based on a dusk attack by the Demons.

Captain Braden stopped in his tracks. "They know we're coming. Someone has betrayed us," he cried.

Haloran shook his head. "We only know they attack at dusk or dawn. That would imply that they travel during the day. Maybe they just can't see very well during the day, like we can't see very well at night. The timing here puts them at the convergence right at dusk. We can turn this to our advantage," he said. "We'll get to the convergence in two candlemarks. We now know when they'll be there. We'll send archers into the trees. Move the horses back toward the Keep with a few of the chargers ready to attack from the rear. Set the men in groups of three or four a few yards into the trees and a very thin screen of men along the road to draw the Demons in. I suspect that they'll come through the trees, probably from the west and south. We knew it was coming. It's just a little quicker."

He's very good. HellReaver gave what Thomas thought of as a mental shrug. *Might as well mount up.*

Thomas's heart started to slow. Fear had tightened his chest, his arms, everything. He hadn't been able to think. "Thank you, Sergeant. Captain, get the men mounted and moving out. Oh, and send a courier back to the Keep to let them know what's happening."

Lady Aeden nodded in approval. "Lord Thomas, I'll stay with you."

"Thank you, Lady. I'm grateful for your help."

She just shook her head and turned to bridle her horse.

Orders were shouted down the line. The column was moving within fifteen minutes.

The men marched along briskly. The road curved to hug the side of the mountain. The mountain's shadow cooled the air further. Small drifts of snow from the frequent short storms at the end of the season lay as a reminder that autumn would soon be gone. The pace fell to a walk. Chain-mail jingled, wagon wheels rumbled and saddles creaked in the cold air.

At the head of the column, Thomas raised his clenched fist and signaled a halt when they reached the convergence of the Caladen and Banuisk rivers. During the summer, white water of the Banuisk surging into the rapids of the Caladen created a dangerous maelstrom of rushing foam over rocks. Now the Banuisk was frozen solid and the Caladen's cold waters flowed sluggishly past the convergence.

"Lady, I think we should cross the Banuisk and set up camp on the other side." He pointed to the left of the track. "That clearing would be perfect. As far as we know, the Demons probably won't cross water. We have at least four candlemarks before dusk."

"I agree, Lord Thomas. That's smart. We can take a break, feed the horses and the men and set up the ambush," replied Aeden.

"Master Sergeant Haloran," Thomas shouted back down the line. Heddwyn tried to spin in a circle under him and he reined the horse sharply around as Haloran cantered up to them.

"We need to cross the Banuisk and set up camp on the other side in that clearing. Hopefully the Demons won't cross and we can use the river as a defense. Could you please make that happen?"

"Yes, my Lord." Haloran bellowed to the staff sergeants in charge of each unit. "Move by units across the river above the convergence." The staff sergeants signaled their understanding. The first unit peeled off from the column and moved toward the frozen riverbank.

Soldiers dismounted and led their horses in single file across the frozen water. Half way through the crossing, the river ice began to groan and snap as weight moved across it. Too many crossing at one time threatened to send them all to the bottom.

Once safely on the other side, the soldiers moved to the clearing and began setting up picket lines for the horses and digging pits for cooking fires.

Stefan and Maccon had accompanied their officers on the trek. They carried saddles and bridles to the wagons and brought back bags of grain for the tethered horses. They each grabbed a brush and started working on brushing out the horses coats. When that chore was done, they each led four horses at a time to the hole that had been chopped in the ice where they could drink.

The last supply wagon rolled down the bank and started across the river. A rumbling cracking followed its progress, but the ice held. Those who stopped to watch heaved sighs of relief and returned to their tasks.

Haloran and two of his men walked to the shore of the Caladen. He gazed across the almost frozen river, mentally arranging the troops for the ambush. He dropped his eyes and looked closely at the bank. He knew he'd seen a submerged ford somewhere around here when he'd scouted during the war. Ah, there it was.

Beneath the water, almost as if a road had been laid, fitted stones formed a broad bed that led toward the opposite shore. They were only half a foot beneath the surface. Haloran drew in his breath with an abrupt gasp as the cold bit into his legs when he walked out into the water, probing with the spear staff that he carried. Stopping and turning toward his men, he beckoned them to him. They splashed through the cold water, following the submerged road.

"Go get a squad of men and cut long poles from tree branches. We need to mark the edges of the ford. Hurry," he urged them.

The men made their way back to shore and trotted to the clearing, shouting out the Master Sergeant's orders. Men hustled to the trees surrounding the camp and began cutting branches. As the branches fell, another squad gathered them and carried them to the shore. Staff sergeants detailed squads to enter the river on either side of the ford and drive the branches into the bottom of the river along the ford edges.

They left the last fifty feet of the ford unmarked. No sense in letting the enemy know exactly where it was.

The cold, wet soldiers made their way back to the camp and the roaring fires that waited to warm them. The camp cook passed out hot tea with whiskey and bowls of stew. This was the last meal before the battle, perhaps the last meal they would ever eat.

Thomas, Aeden, Captain Braden, Master Sergeant Haloran and his staff sergeants met around the fire at the center of the camp.

"The ford is marked, Lord Thomas." Haloran used a long stick to draw a map in the damp earth. "We should move the men across by squads in a candle-mark and set them in a screen along the edge of the forest road to the south and west. Picket five of the horses along the south side of the road to act as shock troops if the need arises."

"Move the archers into the trees on the north. Have them climb as high as they can so they'll be firing down on the Demons," advised Lady Aeden.

Haloran nodded in agreement. He tapped his chin, narrowing his eyes as he stared into the forest. "The scouts can set up deadfalls and snares to slow down the Demon advance there and there." He pointed north and south of the battlefield on the other side of the river. "I wish there was some magical trap that we could set that would thin them out."

Perhaps there is. HellReaver's voice echoed in all of their minds. *Lady Aeden, can you go with the scouts and set magelight to explode when the Demons trip the snares and deadfalls? Make sure that you cut it off from your ki so that it will not drain you.*

Lady Aeden looked at Thomas and HellReaver sheathed at his side with a frown. "I've not done that particular magic before, HellReaver, but I think I can do it."

Good. The sooner the better. I can feel the horde approaching.

The council broke up as everyone scattered to complete their tasks.

Chapter 28

Infantry troops splashed through the cold water between the marker branches that had been placed on either side of the ford. As they clambered up the riverbank on the opposite shore, they hurried to form up and move into the trees on either side of the road. A cold breeze blew down the mountains from the west. Fallen leaves crunched under boots. Men crouched behind snares and deadfalls they had set up to trap the Demons.

Aeden ghosted silently between groups. She set a magelight trigger at each snare and left a portion of magical potential tethered to the trigger. She had gone out five hundred yards and created a trip-line that would alert them to the Demon approach.

Thomas crouched with Captain Braden behind a deadfall close to the ford. Sergeant Haloran had insisted that he be close enough to the river to escape to the other side if things went badly. Aeden slid in beside them, clutching OathKeeper in her fist.

"I saw two of the creatures that Marta described winging along the road. They may be the horde's Smachtmaistir," she muttered to both of them.

"They've taken stations on both sides about two hundred yards beyond the trip-line."

Captain Braden shook his head. "I'll take a squad and try to flank them."

He stood up and waved four soldiers and two archers to join him. They jogged south along the road.

The forest exploded with flashes of magelight and shrieks of Demons as they triggered the magic traps. They had reached the trip-line. Thunder rumbled. Demons poured from the forest on the southwest side of the road. The horses kept in reserve on the road screamed in fear and pain, rearing and kicking out, as Demons leaped on them and started feeding on still living bodies.

Stefan and Maccon pulled their swords and tried to defend the helpless horses. Heddwyn screamed in fear, broke free and galloped frantically away. Stefan swung at the claws that reached for him. He cut one from the Demon's arm, but the other reached past his sword and plunged into his chest. He fell to the ground, dead.

Maccon desperately blocked and blocked but couldn't find any room to attack. The Demons swarmed over him. With a last thrust, he pushed his sword through the chest of a Demon, killing it. The Demon following it slashed down Maccon's face and chest. Blood exploded from his body. He was dead before he hit the ground.

Soldiers grimly swung swords and poleaxes, engaging the Demons by twos and threes. Demon and human blood flew in arches as weapons met flesh. Archers hidden in the trees poured arrows into the writhing mass, targeting Demons as they became separated from the horde. The battle swirled in chaos.

Two hundred yards to the north of the battle, Captain Braden raised his fist, signaling his men to halt. As the sky lit up with mage fire, they could see the figures of two coal black creatures hidden among the evergreen needles, perched on large branches on either side of the road. Braden squinted and tried to make out their shapes, but they were shrouded with some close fitting material. He signaled the archers to target the figures.

The archers drew and loosed their arrows. They flew straight and true. The archers fired again and again, piercing the creatures and skewering them to the trunks of the trees as they spread their membranous wings, trying to take flight.

"Quick," shouted Captain Braden. "Climb up and make sure they're dead."

His troops rushed to the trees and climbed up the trunks. Knives found throats and Demons died.

A shout behind him drew Braden's attention. At least five Demons were rushing toward him, knife-sharp teeth ready to rend and tear. He braced himself for their charge.

The leading two launched themselves and he drove his sword into the chest of the one on the right and his short-sword into the muzzle of the one on the left. He pulled his weapons free and danced over the falling bodies, engaging the next two. He slit throats left and right as they leapt, but he couldn't recover quickly enough to engage the third Demon.

Its teeth fastened on his throat and bore him to the ground. His final sword thrust found its way between the monster's ribs and pierced its heart. He'd fought to his last breath, taking an honor guard of enemies to their deaths.

$$\S \S \S$$

Thomas swung HellReaver with grim purpose; thrust, slice, backhand, again and again and again. Demon blood covered him and dripped from everything. The ground was slippery with it. Bodies lay in clumps of dead Demons and soldiers. Demons circled, feigning attacks and retreating. The stink of sulfur caused him to gag again and again.

As soldiers were killed, surviving Demons joined the attack on Thomas and Aeden. The attacks became more intense. Thomas formed magelight and threw it again and again at the Demons, blinding them.

He faltered as exhaustion set in. Weary muscles started to quiver and refuse to respond. His sword dipped as he panted for breath. A Demon dashed in and knocked the sword from his grasp. As it fell, HellReaver blazed out with a flash of light. The Demons turned away in pain as their eyes were assaulted. Thomas lunged forward and grabbed the sword as it hit the ground. He stabbed up at the Demons not yet recovered from the light, then rolled back to his feet.

A surge of energy rushed into him from HellReaver. He slashed at the two Demons attacking from the right, removing their heads. He followed through with a thrust of his sword to the Demon in front of him. The Demon shrieked, but continued up the sword, eyes locked with his, claws reaching for his throat. Thomas lifted up with a surge of power and disemboweled the creature. Demon blood sprayed.

Demons moved between Aeden and Thomas, forcing her away from the rest of the company. They circled her, then leapt in to attack, clawing and biting. One fastened its jaws on her sword arm, weighing it down and preventing her from swinging OathKeeper. Two more grabbed her leg and started to feed. She screamed in pain. Bodies of Demons bore her to the ground in triumph. OathKeeper lit up with magelight, sending it spearing into the closest Demon.

With a roar like a bear from the north, Thomas raised HellReaver and pointed the sword at the Demons attacking Aeden as he charged to her rescue. Magelight flashed from HellReaver and seared the Demon chewing on her arm. It shrieked and lit up like a torch, burning no matter how the creature twisted and turned and threw itself on the ground to try to extinguish the flames.

Aeden struggled to her feet, slashing at Demons, her legs and arm bleeding badly. She raised Oath-Keeper and called fire from the sky. She lowered the sword and used it like a whip. Wherever it touched, Demons exploded.

Thomas swung again and again in fury, throwing magelight as well as cutting and stabbing, until all of the Demons who had attacked Aeden lay dead. He looked beyond his pile of bodies to see none left standing.

Thomas and Aeden reeled in exhaustion toward each other, clasped each other by the shoulders and slowly folded to the ground. As they sat in a stupor, OathKeeper and HellReaver pulled energy from the earth up into their people. Wounds began to slowly heal as the energy flowed from the swords into their bodies.

Half the company lay dead. The other half staggered to their comrades, checking the wounded and dead, and searching for the living. The archers that Captain Braden had ordered into the trees to bring down the bodies of the odd Demons dragged the corpses to Thomas and threw them on the ground in front of him. Gently they lowered the body of Captain Braden to the ground.

"Lord, Captain Braden is dead," the first archer told him. "He died keeping the Demons off of us while we dragged these abominations out of the trees where they perched. Ain't never seen nothin' like 'em."

§ § §

The Master Sergeant found Thomas and Aeden sitting there, surrounded by dead Demons. He was covered with human blood and Demon gore. He shouted and gestured urgently at two of his men to come help him move them to the bank of the Caladen. The river had kept the Demons from surrounding them and slaughtering everyone.

"My Lord and Lady, you must drink and try to clean up." He cupped his hands and scooped up the frigid water. He held them up to Thomas's mouth. Dazed, it took a moment for Thomas to recognize the water and then he drank. Haloran did the same for Aeden. Soon, both of them were laying on the bank, scooping and drinking on their own.

Exhausted, Thomas rolled to his back on the cold, wet ground with a groan. He slowly pushed himself up on his elbows and upright from there. Aeden did the same.

Thomas looked toward the picket line and it finally hit his brain that none of the horses remained. He pushed himself to his feet and staggered over to the butchery of what had once been twenty horses. He did not see Heddwyn's body and relief surged through him.

He stumbled to the end of the killing field and froze. "No," he cried out in pain when he found Stefan and Maccon. He collapsed to the ground next to their bodies. Tears filled his eyes and he stifled a guttural sob that threatened to overwhelm him.

Haloran sent his men to call in what was left of the company. "You and you," he pointed at two of the survivors, "Wrap the bodies of the Demons in canvas and get them on the wagons. Get others to help do the same for those of ours that lie here. We need to get them back to the Keep."

Thomas stood in stolid silence next to Haloran. "Was this worth it?" he asked. "I lost Captain Braden, Stefan and Maccon. Did we learn anything from this battle?"

"Yes," Haloran responded. "We did. It's going to take more than swords and arrows to save the Keep and the town. It's going to take magic and more people than we have right now to win. This battle

showed us just how little we know about the Demons."
He shook his head in resignation. "Come. Let's gather
up our wounded and dead. This is just the first battle in
what I fear will be a very long war."

Chapter 29

Five long days later, the wagons moved slowly along the road at first light, horses and men weary and despondent. Winter's chill pressed against the earth, slowing movement and thought. As they reached Red Dragon's Keep, the wagons turned south down the road toward the cemetery where the slain would be buried with all honor.

Thomas, Aeden and the remainder of the company rode back into the forecourt that they had left such a short time ago.

The boys, Breanna, and Marta hurried down the steps. Breanna rushed to Thomas and grabbed him in a hug as he dismounted from his borrowed mount. "Are you okay?" her voice wavered. "We knew something was wrong when Heddwyn returned without you."

"I'm all right. We lost half the men and Captain Braden. Maccon and Stefan are dead."

The boys gasped.

"Raina and Marta, Faolan is fine. Thank the Three Gods you came to Red Dragon's Keep when you did. Without him, I think we'd all be dead."

Raina's eyes started to leak tears. Marta swallowed hard and covered her face with both hands, then clasped them together and murmured a short prayer of thanks. Tears dripped from her eyes, but she made no sound.

"Could all of you help with the horses and getting the wounded to the healers? After that, I need a bath and a change of clothes. Let's meet in the great hall in two candlemarks. That should be long enough to get everyone settled."

$$\S \S \S$$

Still tired but much cleaner, Thomas met the others in the great hall. Gregory had ordered mid-meal to be served early. Lady Aeden waited in the arch of the door to the kitchen corridor. Thomas motioned her to meet him at the table.

"Would someone please bring a chair to the table for Lady Aeden? Gregory, please join us."

Cameron jumped up and grabbed two of the chairs sitting along the wall. He bustled back and set them across from Thomas's seat.

"Lady, if you would join me?" Thomas invited. He bowed deeply to her. The others looked on puzzled.

Lady Aeden nodded her thanks and mounted the stairs to the dais. She wore her usual trousers, tunic and low boots. Her fiery red hair flowed freely down her back. She took the chair next to Thomas.

Thomas raised his cup and toasted, "To a hard won battle with thanks to Lady Aeden. Had she not shared her magic, we would not have survived."

Everyone raised their cups and repeated, "Lady Aeden."

Thomas continued, "Tomorrow, we will look to the Keep. We think the Demons will attack here within the fortnight. Everything needs to be ready by then. For now, let's celebrate our first victory and mourn our first loses."

$ $ $

Thomas faced the Demons with only his short sword. HellReaver had been lost during the fight. The Demon in front of him leapt. The one behind him thrust claws into his back. He lunged up out of sleep with a shout, his heart hammering, sweating profusely. *Oh thank the gods, a dream. Just a dream.* He fell back onto the bed.

He felt like he'd not slept at all. He fought with the blankets until they finally released him. Sitting on the edge of his bed, he scrubbed his face with his hands and tried to shake himself to alertness. He looked to the window and saw the first pearl grey light of daybreak washing the sky through the shutters.

He pushed himself to his feet and tried to stretch. His legs rebelled and he almost fell. Every muscle in his body ached. He groaned. The fire in his room hadn't been lit yet. He hobbled over and lit it himself from the fire-keeper. As the logs caught, he sighed. He filled his washbowl with water from the pitcher left there overnight, poured some into his glass, drank it and then another. He washed his face, neck and arms, then worked his cramping legs into trousers and arms into shirt and tunic. He thrust his feet into his house shoes. With slow and deliberate movements, he strapped on HellReaver's sheath.

Good morning, Thomas. It is a good day to be alive.

Good morning HellReaver. If you say so, was Thomas's grumpy response.

HellReaver chuckled.

Thomas walked down the corridor and took the stairs to the great hall. Almost everyone still slept. He heard the clatter of the cooks working in the kitchen, even this early, and walked through the archway and into their domain. Something was always kept simmering for those going to or coming off of watch.

"Good morn, my Lord. How may I serve you?" Restin, the new head cook was short, stout and balding. His apron was covered with spots from checking the food that he cooked. He greeted Thomas, eyeing his sword and sheath with wary caution.

"Good morning...Restin...isn't it? Do you have anything to eat?"

"Right this way my Lord." Restin led Thomas to the warming hearth with its always replenished cauldrons of stew or porridge or soup. A kettle of water and another of tea sat on tripods set at the edge of the banked fire, keeping warm. He grabbed a wooden bowl from the stack to the left of the hearth and a cup from the shelf above. "What would you like, Lord?"

"I'll serve myself. Thanks, Restin." Thomas took the bowl and cup from the cook and dished up some stew from the pot. He grabbed a roll from the basket next to the pot and plopped it onto the stew in his bowl. He put the cup on the hearth and poured himself some hot tea. Turning, he checked that the table sitting in front of the window looking out on the kitchen garden was empty.

He made his way there around tables where bustling cooks, apprentices and skullies worked to get ready for breakfast. He sat down and began to eat.

Aeden slipped into the seat across from him. "Good morning, Lord Thomas. You're up very early."

"Good morning, Lady Aeden. I couldn't sleep. Kept dreaming about Demons." He mopped up some stew with the roll and bit into it. "Please, get some breakfast." He waved toward the warming hearth with the roll and continued chewing.

A small smile tugged at Aeden's lips. She went to the hearth and dished up stew and a cup of tea and returned to the table. They ate in silence until the last bite was gone. Thomas was surprised how much better he felt after eating. He leaned back in his chair and looked around the kitchen as he took another swallow of tea.

He jerked up straight. There should have been barrels of supplies stacked ceiling high around the perimeter of the room. Barrels of flour, corn, water, salted meat. "Restin," he exclaimed.

Restin stopped stirring the pot of beans that he was cooking. He hurried over to the table. "Yes, my Lord?"

"Where are the barrels of supplies that should be lining these walls?"

"My Lord, this is what was here when I took over." Restin gestured at the walls. "I've not seen the usual supplies. I thought that they'd been moved to provide more space for our work. Was I mistaken?"

"Lady, did you hear anything about moving supplies?" he asked Aeden.

She shook her head. "No. I think we'd better check with Gregory, right now."

"Restin, check with everyone on staff and see if they know what happened to the supplies. Let me know as soon as you find out. We'll find Gregory."

They pushed back their chairs from the table and strode from the kitchen.

Gregory jumped to his feet as Thomas and Aeden burst through the doors to his office.

"What is it?" he exclaimed in alarm.

"What happened to the supplies that should be lining the walls of the kitchen and the halls?" Thomas almost shouted. Aeden laid a calming hand on his shoulder.

"Ah." Gregory sighed with relief. "I've ordered all of the supplies that are already here moved to the cellars. After you killed the seleigh soren, we were able to use that area again. Once it's full, we'll start using the halls and kitchen.

"Thank the gods!"

You are right, young Thomas. Something feels off. Send men to check the lower levels. HellReaver spoke to all of them.

Gregory started at the voice in his mind. He shook his head. "I'll never get used to that."

"Send a squad of guards to check the supplies, Gregory."

"Yes, my Lord. Jago, front!"

Jago hurried across the hallway into the office.

"Get a squad of soldiers and check the supplies in the undercroft," Gregory ordered. Jago paused, then turned and jogged from the room. Gregory, Thomas and Aeden exchanged a long look.

HellReaver spoke. *That young man is a traitor.*

Thomas moved to the door and peered quickly around the door frame. Jago stood at the end of the corridor, talking into some kind of cube. Aeden ducked down below Thomas and looked the same way.

"Hold." Thomas straightened and stepped into the hall. Power beat through his blood as he issued his command.

Jago froze in the act of putting the cube back into his pocket.

Aeden flowed out of the door and over to Jago. Thomas and Gregory followed her. She leaned forward to inspect the cube.

"This is a communication device. He was probably contacting someone with the Demons." She reached out and plucked it from Jago' frozen fingers.

Thomas looked into Jago' eyes and saw fear and panic as he struggled to break free.

Aeden frowned in thought. She handed the cube to Thomas. It felt like crystal, perhaps made of quartz that came from the gold mines riddling the mountains surrounding the valley. It felt oily to his touch.

Perhaps treated with something or manipulated magically? Aeden spoke to OathKeeper and HellReaver.

I think yes. There is a high level spell permeating this object, responded OathKeeper.

"Thomas, would you and HellReaver please place a shield around this object? I want to see if I can use it to locate the receiver. I have several tracking spells I'd like to try."

Thomas reached out with his mind and created a bubble around the device. He felt HellReaver and Oath-Keeper add their power to the spell. Thomas closed it off with a deft twist of his mind and handed the enclosed crystal back to Aeden.

Gregory, Aeden and Thomas turned and looked at Jago. Thomas released him from his stasis with a touch of his mind. Jago made a move as if to run. His shoulders slumped in defeat. There was nowhere to run to.

Gregory shook his head. "I can't believe this. First Jalyn and now you? How far does the rot spread?"

Thomas stared at Jago. He'd grown up with him. This betrayal hurt more than the others. Another layer of numbness surrounded his feelings. The chill in the corridor echoed his emotions.

"Lady Aeden, would you please go and find whoever is on duty and send troops to check on the supplies and four soldiers to take Jago to the cells? I think those doing the checking might need a mage with them. Something doesn't feel right about any of this. I'd ask HellReaver to bespeak them, but that might cause more panic."

Aeden nodded and hurried down the corridor. Thomas put his hand on HellReaver's pommel and nodded toward Gregory's office.

"Move," he growled to Jago.

Aeden returned in a short while. "We couldn't find anything sinister in the cellars among the supplies. I can feel something - I just can't tell what," she reported. The guards arrived and removed Jago in chains, marching him to the former supply room that had become the Keep's holding cell.

"Lady Aeden, you decide what to do with him. I need to talk with Haloran about setting up defenses," Thomas told her. Aeden looked startled and then nodded in agreement.

§ § §

Thomas didn't bother to take his dinner to the head table to eat. He was just too tired. He'd spent the entire day with Haloran and his military staff, working out the defenses for the Keep. Lady Aeden joined them after mid-meal to share her thoughts on defensive measures.

He made his way to the table closest to the pitchers of water and sat on the trestle table bench. He was thirsty, too. He picked up the wooden spoon he'd stuck in the thick stew the cooks served for dinner. Slices of fresh bread rested on platters that sat at the center of each table. He grabbed two and began to spoon the stew into his mouth. He'd been using magic continuously and hadn't taken the time to eat enough to replace the energy that he'd lost. Now was his chance.

Thomas looked around the room as he continued to eat. Magelight mounted on ornate brackets hung on chains depending from the ceiling. While not bright, they gave enough light to see by. He watched the captain of the guard sitting with the blacksmith and listened while they talked about the best way to create a fuller on a sword. The blacksmith's hands, while clean, were forever blackened by the charcoal used in his trade.

The table behind him was filled with the women who worked in the laundry every day. They smelled of lye soap and chattered among themselves.

Thomas glanced at the tapestries covering the walls and was caught by the view of the one on the north wall to his left. Sitting in this location gave him an entirely different perception of the warhorses and knights that galloped across the fields of grain. He'd never noticed the farmers' cottages in the background when he looked at it from the head table.

He looked at the other tapestries as he ate. Each one held something that he'd not seen before. Maybe he was more sensitive to the differences that he noticed now. He looked toward the fireplace and watched as Owen and Breanna ate their meals. He'd never been aware how on display anyone who sat at that table was. He felt oddly embarrassed.

His eyes traced the outline of the fireplace and watched as light and shadow chased themselves across its sides and back. His eyes were drawn to the mural that graced the wall above the mantle topping the fireplace.

Images of Dragons soared above the massacre of Demons and humans taking place below them. A depiction of the sun sent rays of light flowing down over the battlefield. The rays were represented by circles filled with jewels.

Thomas's eyes stopped at one of the circles. A half arc of stone with jewels running from the center to the rim on two sides sent a shock through his system. He almost gasped aloud, and then furtively glanced around. No one had noticed.

He finished his stew without tasting it, got up and returned the wooden bowl, spoon and cup to the basket that sat at the end of the table. He went in search of Lady Aeden.

He found her in her quarters behind the salle. She sat on a saddle chair, sharpening OathKeeper. A tray filled with empty dishes sat outside the door, waiting for the return of the skully who had brought her dinner from the kitchen.

"Lady Aeden," he gasped. "I think I found it!" He lowered his voice to a whisper. "The amulet!"

Aeden jerked to her feet, grasping OathKeeper to keep him from falling to the ground.

"Where?" she demanded.

"The mural above the great hall fireplace," he responded. He turned to rush back to the room, but she grabbed his arm and stopped his movement.

"No. This needs to be done when no one is around. Here. Sit. She tossed the tunic and trousers on the stool next to her saddle chair in the basket beside the door. Thomas walked over and perched on the stool. He vibrated with tension.

"You're right. I just want to see if it is the Dragon amulet and move it to safety," he gulped.

Aeden poured a mug of water from a pitcher on her table and handed it to Thomas.

"Drink this. It will help calm you down. Did anyone notice what you were doing?" she asked.

"I don't think so. I checked and nobody looked interested in me. I might have missed it though." He shook his head. "Right in front of us all this time. We need to get it out."

"Slow down, Lord Thomas," Aeden snapped at him. "No one has discovered it since it was put there. I think it is safe enough for now."

"Right, right. We'll have to wait until midnight or later, when no one is around."

They sat in silence for some time.

"So, how did you see it?" Aeden asked him.

"I was eating dinner below the salt," he replied. "I've not been eating enough after doing magic and I was really hungry. I just grabbed and sat and started eating. I started looking at the tapestries and listening to people. I looked at the mural, and the amulet almost jumped out at me. It's in the rays of light from the sun above the King killing the Demon that tried to eviscerate him."

Aeden looked at the far wall, as if picturing the mural in her mind.

"I know exactly where you're talking about," she said. "I want to go see it myself."

They filled the time with talk about magic and how it could be used to fight the Demons and came up with several ideas to try at the next training session. Thomas went to the door to check for signs that the Keep was settling for the evening so often that Aeden irritably told him to stop and sit quietly.

Time passed with agonizing slowness. Finally, Aeden judged that almost everyone had retired for the night. The two of them moved quietly along the walk and entered the kitchen. The fires were banked for the night and covered bowls filled with bread dough set to rise for breakfast rested on tables in the center of the room.

Aeden followed Thomas into the great hall and walked to its center. They turned and looked at the mural painted above the fireplace. The amulet almost shouted its presence. They looked at each other, then walked to the fireplace and looked up. Real gems instead of glass droplets winked in the dim light.

"You're right, Lord Thomas. It's the amulet, hidden in plain sight." Aeden sighed. "We can't do anything about it now. We'll get Gregory in the morning and figure out what to do. Best to try and sleep now and deal with it then." She grinned wryly. "I know it won't be easy. Try anyway."

"Yes Lady." Thomas was suddenly exhausted. "I'll go now. Meet in the kitchen after breakfast?" he asked.

"See you then," she responded.

$$\$ \, \$ \, \$$

Aeden watched as he left the room and mounted the stairs. She gazed at the amulet for a short time, thinking about its history. Shaking her head, she turned and made her way back to her own bed.

$$\$ \, \$ \, \$$

Thomas fell asleep quickly, but awoke time and again, jerked out of sleep by the knowledge that they had found the amulet. Finally he gave up, dressed and went down to breakfast.

Aeden pointed out the Dragon amulet in the painted mural above the fireplace to Gregory with furtive gestures before they met Thomas in the kitchen. Gregory was by turns elated and apprehensive. He followed Aeden and Thomas up to the Library.

"I'm not sure that we shouldn't just leave it where it is. It's been safe there for who knows how long," Gregory started the conversation as they took their seats around the table. Bright sunshine filled the room with light.

"I've been trying to think of a safer place, but I can't. I agree with Gregory," Aeden added.

"The only problem I see is that we need to be able to remove it quickly if the Demons come and it looks like the Keep might fall," Thomas answered.

"There's that," Gregory responded.

"I've got a confession to make and I hope it doesn't make you too mad with me." Embarrassed, Thomas cleared his throat and look everywhere but at them.

"There's a secret passage within the walls of the Tower. One of the branches lies right behind the mural above the great hall fireplace. There is even a loose stone that you can remove so you can hear what is being said and see who is in the room, if they stand in the right place. I don't know where on the mural wall it is, but we can check it and see if it's anywhere near the amulet." He gave his confession in a hurried mumble, wanting to get it all out at once.

Aeden and Gregory sat in stunned silence.

"I didn't want anyone else to know. I found it by accident last year. One of the doors is in my room. It's why I've been able to understand what's been going on in the Keep," he pleaded for understanding. "I just wish I'd found out about Jalyn before she did anything," he finished.

"Hmmm," said Aeden into the quiet of the room.

Gregory said nothing, just stared at him for long moments. "That's a lot to take in. Have you mapped it?"

"I...No, I haven't seen it all. I've tried to map it. I think only the Duke is supposed to know about it and someone forgot to tell my father. He's never said a word to me," Thomas answered. "I'm going to have to ask for your oaths to keep it a secret."

"Of course," Gregory and Aeden spoke at the same time.

"Gregory, you and I will adjourn to the great hall. Thomas, you go to the fireplace wall and see if you can locate the amulet from that side," She stood and so did Gregory. "If you can't tell, come and get us and we'll figure something out."

Thomas nodded his head mutely.

"Thank you for telling us, Thomas. There's no other way to get to the amulet without everyone knowing. You've done the right thing." She put a hand on Gregory's arm and drew him out of the Library.

Well, that was interesting. HellReaver spoke in his mind. *I knew about the passage, but not that you did. This makes the task much easier.*

Thomas slapped the table in frustration. *Did you know about the amulet?*

No. It was made before my creation. I know only what you do from the records.

Thomas's disgruntlement eased a little.

$ $ $

He left the Library and made his way to his room. He locked the door with the iron pin through the hasp. He moved to the side of his fireplace and pressed out the pattern, opening the passage door. Lighting his small lantern, he moved unerringly through the maze and stopped behind the mural.

He moved the lantern along the wall, looking for the loose stone. There it was. He set the lantern on the floor and dimmed its light. He carefully rocked the stone from its bed. As he drew it out, he turned it over. It was the amulet, set with real jewels, not glass gems. He took a breath in wonder. Nothing gave away its power as he handled it. He hadn't even guessed that there was anything different about it. He'd simply removed the stone and set it on the floor when he'd used this vantage point to listen to the wisdom of his elders.

This makes our task of guarding the amulet much easier, young Thomas. HellReaver sounded pleased.

Carefully, Thomas replaced the stone with slow steady pressure. Lifting the lantern, he checked that everything was in its place and returned to his room. He closed the passage door and swept the dust from in front of the panel. He blew out the lantern and set it on the mantle. He left the room.

$ $ $

Thomas met Aeden and Gregory in the great hall. They watched him with solemn faces as he approached.

"Let's go to my office," Gregory said with a curt nod.

Thomas followed them down the hall. Gregory closed the door after they entered, then turned to Thomas and grinned. Aeden's grin was just as wide.

"Well done, my Lord. We saw the stone disappear, but no one else did. Then it reappeared. It's only visible if you are looking right at it." Gregory was exultant.

"We don't need to move it at all now. Only if the Keep is going to fall," added Aeden.

Thomas nodded in agreement.

"We tell no one," he added in reminder. "I want to have a meeting with everyone to plan the defense of the Keep. I need to get something from the Library. Let's all meet in the Solar in half a candlemark."

Chapter 30

Gregory found Owen and Breanna at weapons practice. The cousins and Marta, as well as Sergeant Haloran, were doing an inventory of arrows and pitch balls. He passed on Thomas's request and they all met in the Solar around the large ornately carved table that served Thomas's mother for everything from cutting fabric to repairing armor. Its legs were carved into Dragons and its top was gouged and scarred. It was sanded smooth at least twice a year.

Thomas walked in with rolled plans for each floor of the Keep that he'd found in the Library. He unrolled each one on the table.

"Grab something to weigh down each corner," he told everyone.

Books and crystals and statues were pulled down from shelves for weights. Breanna brought a rock that was used as the doorstop. When corners were weighted, everyone bent forward to look. Thomas waved his hand over the plans.

"Sergeant Haloran, I know you've assigned troops to defend each floor of the Tower if the Demons get in. Here's my thought. I'd like all of us to help with that.

Teams of two, and their Swords of Light, will patrol each level of the Keep with the soldiers, watching for Demons coming through the portals."

He pointed at each floor on the plans. "Breanna and Cameron, you're a team on the second level. Evan and Owen, you're a team on the third level. Marta, you're in charge of the interior defense. You roam between floors, checking each team."

"Sergeant Haloran, what do you think?"

The sergeant crossed his arms, and then put his chin in his hand in thought. "It's a good plan, Lord Thomas. We'll need everyone, including your Swords, to defend the Tower. I'd recommend assigning six soldiers to the fourth floor. Evan and Owen can check in with them periodically. They'll need the help when the Demons come through the portals to attack."

Thomas nodded in agreement. "I like it. Let's get everything ready. I want to get as many villagers inside the inner walls as possible. The walls need to be manned at all times and the villagers can help with that. Sergeant, can you see to it?"

Haloran nodded.

"All of you need to know we caught Jago communicating through some kind of device with the Demons." He shook his head and muttered, "I still can't believe it."

Stunned silence filled the room.

"Why would he betray us?" Breanna whispered. Aeden stepped over to her side and put her arm around Breanna's shoulders.

"Some people are weak and think that they will gain strength and be more powerful by serving another master. Some do it for the thrill. It doesn't matter why. We'll never know for sure. What really matters is the damage that he has done," Aeden told her.

Thomas frowned and looked around the table. "We're going to have to do it again, darn it! Another chore on the list of things to be done."

"What?" asked Owen.

"Check the whole Keep again for portals and magical traps. Okay. Owen and Evan, take the third floor. Ask your swords to help. Breanna and Cameron, take the second floor. Marta and I will check here and in the undercroft. We'll meet in the armory and do a sweep there, then through the rest of the Keep grounds. Do you all remember how to isolate and destroy anything you find?" Everyone nodded.

"Good. Let's go."

The boys left in a clump. Haloran walked out of the Solar with Aeden.

Thomas gathered the plans and rolled them into a cylinder. He looked out the east windows at the gathering clouds and the dimming light as the sun slowly set, his mind far away, thinking of his parents. *I wonder if Captain Mathin has found them yet.* No report had arrived since Mathin had ridden out of the Keep.

He shook his head and turned to find the room empty but for Marta.

"My Lord, I wanted to fill you in about the cousins' training. They are doing really well. Our ..." she paused to search for the right term, "sword companions...have been helping them a lot. Even Breanna can defend and attack. I'm pretty surprised."

Thomas grinned. "Quite a change from trying to teach all alone, isn't it? HellReaver did the same for me. Teaching Owen actually helped me a lot. Let's get this floor swept for Dark magic and then check the undercroft again."

"Yes, Lord."

"And call me Thomas when no one else is around. I still look around for my Father when I hear 'Lord'."

"Okay, Thomas," Marta said slowly. She avoided looking at him. "This room at least is clear. Hell-Scream told me that she's felt something in the kitchen hallway."

"Lead on. The sooner we start, the quicker we finish." He gestured toward the doorway with a grand sweep of his arm.

Chapter 31

Breanna shivered. She felt a cold prickle of fear slither down her spine. Goosebumps rose on her arms. She and Cameron were searching every room on the second floor - the family's floor. They had been through six of the rooms so far.

"Cameron, wait! Something's here," she hissed.

Cameron glanced at her and let his eyes run along the corridor that they had just stepped into from her father's room. Something moved along the wall on the floor. He reached out and grabbed Breanna's arm, nodding his head at the large rat scurrying down the hall.

"Let's follow," he whispered. "This might be the break we need."

They trailed the rat, and watched as it turned the corner into Evan's room. They crept to the door frame and Cameron slowly pushed one eye past the wood until he could see into the room. Breanna edged her head past the frame below his.

The rat sat up in the middle of the room, utterly still, holding something in its jaws, its back to them. Its fur was thin and patchy. A long thin grey naked tail stretched out behind. It looked sick. Its head turned jerkily from right to left. It suddenly scuttled toward the large wooden wardrobe that held Evan's clothes and ran behind it.

Cameron drew GhostWalker from his scabbard. Breanna drew SunWalker. They charged through the door and over to opposite sides of the wardrobe. Cameron pressed his eye to the gap between the wall and the back of the wardrobe. Breanna did the same on the other side. The rat was up on its hind legs leaning its front paws against the wall, pressing the object that it held against it with its snout. Cameron thrust GhostWalker toward the rat. Light flared and there was a tiny shriek as the sword's magic engulfed it. Breanna pushed SunWalker toward the disk on the wall, then behind it, popping it off. She used the sword to pull the disk along the floor toward her.

"That's how they are getting in here!" Cameron came around to her side of the wardrobe and looked at the disk. "Maybe we can put a spell on it and take it to Lady Aeden? We need to tell everyone how they are getting in."

"SunWalker? Can you do that?" Breanna asked.

Yes. Touch my blade to the disk.

A shimmer of light covered the disk in a small bubble. Cameron reached down and picked it up. "Come on. Let's get this to Lady Aeden."

$$\$ \$ \$$$

They hurried out of the room and down the corridor to the stairs that descended to the great hall. Taking the stairs as fast as they could, they charged across the hall and out to the forecourt. Aeden and

Haloran stood before a group of villagers, explaining what they would need to do to defend the Keep. Aeden's eyes jerked to the children and she turned as they ran up.

"What is it?" she asked, frowning in concern.

"There was a rat that ran into Evan's room." Breanna spoke between gasps for breath. "We killed it, and pried this off the wall. SunWalker put a shield around it so you could see."

"That's how the portals are getting into the Keep!" Cameron panted. He handed the shielded disk to Aeden as she held out her hand.

"Good work, you two," she exclaimed. "This explains much." Snow started to drift down from the lowering sky. "Sergeant Haloran, could you finish assigning these good people to watch the walls, and then join us in the great hall? I'll gather the others."

"Of course, my Lady." He turned to the forty men and women who would take this shift of the watch. They held pikes, and bows, and arrows, as well as pitchforks and rusty swords that they had brought with them from their homes and Steadings. "Let's get up on the wall and I'll have the corporal-in-charge show you where to stand and what to watch for."

The forty turned and marched as best they could after Haloran. They showed their pride in sharing the defense of the Keep with straight backs and ordered steps. Aeden watched them with sorrow in her heart. She hoped that most of them would be alive after the Demons attacked, but she knew how close it was going to be.

She shook her head and turned toward the Keep. "Come on. Let's get to a table inside. OathKeeper, can you please bespeak everyone and ask them to come here?"

Thomas and Marta, Evan and Owen, and finally Haloran entered the great hall from three different directions. Haloran was followed by twenty soldiers he had assigned to follow the teams during any battle in the Tower.

"What is it?" demanded Thomas.

"Thanks to Cameron and Breanna, we now know how the portals are getting into the Keep. Whoever is commanding the Demon hordes is using rats to place the portals within our walls." Aeden spoke grimly and gestured toward the table where she had placed the disk within its magical shield.

"Can you follow the spell back to its maker?" Haloran asked.

"I thought to try it now with the help of all of you. Come, around the table and place your swords like this beside the disk." Aeden laid OathKeeper next to it. Thomas laid HellReaver at an angle across Oath-Keeper. The others laid their swords as Aeden directed until they lay in a star shape enclosing the disk.

"Sergeant Haloran, please keep everyone away until this is done."

Aeden closed her eyes and called on her power. She drew as well on the power of the Swords of Light and their wielders. Above the star, a shimmering mist began to form. Within the mist a wavering image took shape.

"This is the spellcaster," she growled. "Do any of you recognize him?"

Those in the circle shook their heads. Haloran turned to look and all the blood drained from his face.

"I know that man!" he exclaimed. "That's Mannan. He's one of the King's councilors. He rallied the Cailleachs to help defeat the Sabhdans of Fasach in the last human war. Even then, he was a powerful mage."

Aeden's eyebrows rose as her eyes widened. "Oh, really?"

She frowned, and her jaw tightened. "Why does it seem that evil always emanates from Fasach? It's something to think about." She crossed her arms and stood in deep thought. Finally she shook her head and looked at the others. "We'll have to search for more of the portals."

Shouts erupted in the forecourt just outside the great doors.

Chapter 32

Screams of fear and pain joined the cacophony. Everyone in the hall rushed toward the doors.

"No!" shouted Aeden. "Take your swords and get to your assigned defenses. The attack has begun. Watch for intruders in the corridors. Haloran, get the soldiers in here to protect each group." She ran out of the doors to the forecourt.

Cameron and Breanna, Evan and Owen, Thomas and Marta charged back to the table and grabbed up their swords. The teams raced up the staircase to their corridors. Haloran shouted for the soldiers he had told to stand by and sent them chasing the teams.

§§§

Thomas and Marta hurried down the corridor to the kitchen and Gregory's office, waiting for the tingle that would signal a portal had been opened. The hair on the back of Thomas's neck rose and he felt the tingle sweep his body. He brought HellReaver up in guard position as he slowed to a stop. Marta raised HellScream as well, and stood at his side.

Thomas! Beware! HellReaver warned.

The door to Jago's office disintegrated into kindling as a monstrous creature filled its frame. Thomas and Marta reeled back against the wall, away from it.

Black as night, the Demon seemed to smoke as waves of heat rose from its body. Thomas recovered first. His lips drew back exposing his teeth and he snarled. He lowered HellReaver and thrust the Sword of Light into the belly of the Demon. Marta swung HellScream and sliced through the creature's shoulder, severing its taloned arm.

Thomas pulled HellReaver back, and then spun in a graceful circle, beheading the Demon, ending its keening shrieks. Five of the soldiers assigned as Thomas's bodyguards finally arrived and slipped past them, facing down the corridor, ready to take on anything else that attacked.

"I'd better get outside to the forecourt with Aeden," Thomas told Marta as he wiped HellReaver on the body of the fallen Demon. He pointed down the corridor with his Sword of Light. "You five," he nodded at the soldiers, "patrol this corridor and the great hall," he ordered the soldiers. "Marta, check in with each team." He turned and left her there.

$$\$\,\$\,\$$

Cameron and Breanna surged into the family corridor from the stairwell with their swords already raised in front of them. Two Demons and a winged Smachtmaistir attacked from both sides.

The six soldiers assigned to their level fought back to back, protecting each other from the Demons snapping at arms and legs and throats.

Cameron frantically raised his blade to block claws that slashed at his face.

Breanna shrieked as the Smachtmaistir raked her left arm from shoulder to elbow. She slashed her blade in a wild swing and decapitated the Demon.

Cameron thrust GhostWalker through the breast-bone of the Demon attacking him. It squalled and pushed itself up the blade, talons reaching for him. He kicked it off of the sword and, with a shout of pure rage, raised GhostWalker over his head and brought the blade down on the Demon's head with every ounce of strength he possessed.

Breanna screamed in anger and pain and attacked the last Demon as it sprang toward Cameron's back. She drove SunWalker through its back, then jerked up and out through its shoulder. She swung the sword back in a great arc and took its head.

The soldiers were down, four killed and two wounded. The Demons they'd fought lay dead in pools of blood and pieces of Demon.

Cameron pulled Breanna against his side, keeping her from collapsing in shock and pain. "Come on. We need to get that bandaged and be ready for more attacks."

He pulled her into the bathing room where towels were neatly stacked. He laid down his sword on the bench against the wall. He took Breanna's blade from unresisting fingers and did the same with it. He grabbed a cloth and clamped it to Breanna's arm. "Hold this tight," he said, his stomach turning at all of the blood flowing down her arm.

He grabbed a drying sheet and ripped it into several thin strips, then wound them around Breanna's towel-covered arm, tying the ends at her shoulder. "Can you still fight?" he asked, afraid her answer would be no.

"I think I can," she said shakily. "SunWalker, can you help me?"

Yes, I will. The sword sent energy flowing into Breanna. "Let's get back out there," she muttered.

Four soldiers surged up the stairs and jerked to a stop by the human and Demon bodies.

Cameron and Breanna staggered out of the bathing room, swords raised, ready to fight on.

"Looks like you didn't need much help," the corporal in charge of the squad remarked dryly, noting the wounds and shredded bloody clothes on the children, the dead and wounded soldiers and the dead Demons.

"I think you need to stay on this level and guard against any more Demons coming through the portals," Cameron suggested to the corporal.

$§§§$

Owen and Evan met up with the six soldiers assigned to their team on the third floor. They both saw mangy rats scurrying down the hall at the same time and sprang after them. The grey creatures almost blended in with the stone walls. They ran toward the Solar and several split off from the main group to run into the rooms lining the corridor. Immediately Demons transported through the portals and the rats died.

Evan leapt right and Owen leapt left, skewering Demons. A Smachtmaistir came through the portal. Both of them swung their swords and cut it in half before it could unfurl its wings.

More Demons poured from the portals. The soldiers, Evan and Owen were fully engaged, swinging, thrusting, hacking - trying to keep the monsters from getting past them.

Five Demons and another Smachtmaistir fought past them and raced down the stairs. They met Marta, Cameron, and Breanna coming up.

Screams of rage echoed up the stairwell. Marta, Cameron and Breanna fought up the stairs. The going was difficult because of the stairwell's turn to the right. They couldn't engage the Demons and Smachtmaistir until the enemy were right on top of the trio. Swords flamed and incinerated Demons.

The children smashed their way through the Demons, leaving the injured to be dispatched by the soldiers responding from the floor below to the battle. They joined Owen, Evan and the rest of the third floor soldiers in their fight.

They thrust and hacked and sliced until every Demon lay dead.

Panting from exertion, the combatants leaned against furniture or walls, covered with blood, both Demon and their own. Not one of the humans escaped without injury.

§ § §

Thomas ran down the stairs to the forecourt. The sun lay low on the horizon, about to fall behind the mountains. Demons attacked the walls, climbing them and killing the defenders at the top. Flying

Demons dropped huge boulders onto the walls and breached them in two places. Smachtmaistirs hovered in the air, somehow directing the flood of Demons assaulting the Keep.

Demons poured through the breaches, onto the ramparts and over the inner walls. Dead and dying villagers and Demons littered the ramparts, stairs, and grounds. Demons stopped at the dead bodies and started to eat them as others scrambled past, looking for easy prey.

Defenders threw dead Demons over the walls to distract those who were trying to climb up the outside. Some of the Demons looked oddly human.

Soldiers battled Demons in the forecourt. Thomas charged into the middle of the battle, swinging HellReaver in great arcs, slicing arms and legs, torsos and faces, as if he were possessed. Demons fell as he pushed toward Aeden. Simon followed at his back, clumsily trying to protect him with a short sword.

Haloran ran at the Demons attacking the defenders on the stairs. He helped the desperate men and women drive the Demons back down into the forecourt.

Thomas raised his hand and called magefire. He threw the glowing ball of fire into the face of a Demon that reached for his throat. The Demon shrieked and fell to the ground, clawing at its face. Thomas drove HellReaver through its heart, pulled back and swung, taking its head.

He whirled around at a scream of agony behind him. He shouted in horror. Demon claws impaled Simon. The huge Demon lifted his writhing body into the air. Simon shrieked again. Thomas charged forward and thrust

HellReaver through the Demon's body. Another Demon grabbed Simon's body as it fell and began to feed. Rage filled Thomas's body. He screamed in battle fury and charged at the Demon. The Demon snarled soundlessly in the noise of battle and jumped to attack him. Thomas whirled HellReaver over his head and slashed the Demon's head from its body.

The forecourt was filled with struggling humans and attacking Demons. Human defenders fell as more Demons poured into the battle.

Aeden danced and ducked, whirled and lunged, OathKeeper a scythe of steel, killing Demons and their masters, the Smachtmaistirs, as they tried to overwhelm her with numbers. She hurled magefire at faces, arms and torsos, lighting up Demons to burn to death. More and more of the Demons converged on her.

A Smachtmaistir ripped OathKeeper from her hand. Demons clawed her from throat to belly. They clung to both legs with their claws and teeth. A Demon fastened its teeth on her arm, bearing her to the ground. Another twisted past her magefire and dug razor sharp claws into the opposite arm while ripping at her belly with its hind feet.

OathKeeper, lying on the ground at Aeden's head, flared with magefire. The Sword blazed brightly, sending its fire into the Demons ravaging Aeden's arms. The Demons lit up like torches.

Aeden screamed in pain and fear and rage. She lurched up to her feet, kicking at the Demons on her legs, raised her hands and face to the sky and shrieked to power.

The sky darkened as an inrushing of smoke, black fog and howling wind created a tornado of force around her.

Every eye was riveted on the tornado. Fighting stopped as if everyone had been paralyzed. Demons squalled in sudden fear and tried to retreat. The tornado grew larger, sending Demons flying into the walls of the Keep and smashing into the ground. The tornado roared as it lifted away.

A huge red Dragon, three times taller than a man, stood in Aeden's place, tail lashing, eyes red as flame, mouth agape, showing rows of jagged teeth ready to rend and tear. A row of bony spikes traced its backbone to the very end of its tail. That tail lashed, sending Demons cartwheeling into the swords of the defenders.

The scales edged in gold that covered its body glistened. Its neck snaked forward as it swung toward the closest knot of Demons. The frill anchored behind its head lifted and expanded, making the red Dragon's head look twice its size. Huge sharp teeth clamped down on the cluster of Demons trying to attack its forelegs. It flung the shrieking mass against the Keep wall, shattering bodies and splattering blood.

Red as fire, the Dragon reared onto its hind legs, translucent wings extended, foreclaws lashing out again and again. Its sinuous neck writhed back as it inhaled a great lungful of air. Lunged forward, flames erupted from its mouth. It swung its head from side to side, incinerating Demons and their masters with incandescent Dragon fire. Where it touched, none escaped.

Thomas saw what was coming and anchored his ki into the earth. He raised a shield and extended it over the soldiers and villagers that stood in the Dragon's path. The fire washed around Thomas and the remaining defenders, parted by his hastily constructed shield, sparing them its ravening, blistering heat.

The forecourt was clear of Demons. The Dragon gave a great bellow and launched itself to the top of the Keep wall. Massive jaws clamped down on Demons scrambling away and crunched. Eyes glittering, it peered over the wall. Another inhale and flames ignited and danced along the Demons climbing the walls on the outside of the Keep. Winged Demons and Smachtmaistirs dove at the Dragon, talons raking its back and neck without effect. It launched itself off the wall and mighty wings drove it high above the Demons. Shrieking, it plummeted toward the ground and the hovering Demons.

The red Dragon swept its head from side to side as waves of fire burst from its throat. Wings and legs and bodies flamed. Demons died twisting and screaming, falling to the earth and disintegrating on impact. It chased those desperately trying to escape and bathed them with its fire. At last, the sky was clear. The Dragon glided above the Keep wall, looking for more Demons to kill.

Finally it tilted its wings and backwinged to land in the forecourt.

Thomas slowly straightened, lowered his sword and stood stunned, not sure what to say or do. The others slowly rose to their feet. Thomas released his shield abruptly. Even HellReaver was silent.

§ § §

The Red Dragon shifted uneasily. *What am I supposed to do now?*

She flung her head toward the sky and bugled.

The whirlwind formed about her, less intense this time, hiding her magnificent shape. As it dissipated, Lady Aeden stood in the Dragon's place.

She fell to her knees in shock. She remembered everything: the reason for her long exile; her father, the other Dragons.

Thomas thumped wearily to the ground next to her. "Thank you, Lady Aeden. Is that your name? Why didn't you tell us?"

Hush, young Thomas. The Dragon has returned and now remembers her past. You would do well to give her time.

"It's all right, HellReaver. Thomas, I didn't know myself until the whirlwind took me. I understand so much more now." She shook her head in disbelief and covered her face with her hands. She raised her head and looked at Thomas, eyes as fierce as those of the Dragon she was.

"I will always fight with you, Thomas. You and yours are my children."

§ § §

All of the defenders from the interior of the Keep filtered out into the forecourt as the last Demons fell and news of the victory spread. Bodies of Demons and humans littered the ground. Marta and the children sat in a huddle on the steps into the Keep, wounded and exhausted, hardly able to think. Haloran, Raina, and their sons leaned against the Keep wall next to the doors. Others squatted in groups or simply laid out flat on the ground.

Villagers moved among them, helping the wounded and ladling out cups of water and wine. Thomas accepted a cup from a little girl covered with soot from the Dragon's fire. She had obviously been behind the shield he had created. She smiled at him, her teeth brilliant as she handed him the cup.

"Thank you, Lord Thomas, for saving me." Thomas patted her on her shoulder. "You're welcome," he rumbled to her. He walked up the steps and turned to the others in the forecourt.

"All of you, I have something everyone needs to know." Thomas's voice was hoarse, but he projected it as well as he could. "Lady Aeden is a Dragon." He shook his head, still not believing what he was saying. The water in his cup almost spilled as his hand trembled with weariness. "Without her help, the Keep would have been lost in this first battle."

"What?!"

"What are you talking about?"

"How could she be a Dragon? She's always been here!" A babble of questions and exclamations broke out among those who had not been in the forecourt for the battle.

Thomas raised his hand for quiet.

Let her tell her story. OathKeeper shocked everyone into silence. Aeden's sword seldom spoke to others.

"Thank you, OathKeeper," Aeden said dryly.

She stood up from where she had been kneeling, partially supported by the Keep wall and walked up the stairs to stand beside Thomas.

"My name is Fire and I am a Dragon. Long ago my race withdrew to the Dragon Lands far to the north and west. My father is King of the Dragons. He saw a future after the last Demon War where Dragons came to rule humans. Humans eventually revolted against that rule.

He gave each of us a choice: withdraw and leave off all contact with humans or lose all knowledge of what we are and become simply human mages with no ability to change. I chose the latter. Only three of us so chose."

She leaned on OathKeeper and gazed at the farthest wall of the Keep, her mind far away, lost in her past. She returned with a start.

"Long ago, the Arachs held Red Dragon's Keep when Dragons came to the aid of humans against the Ciardha Demons in the first Demon war. At the end of that war, the Arachs, called Dread Lords and Tiarna Geal, or Lords of Light, were offered the rule of Ard An Tir. They declined and chose to withdraw to their home, to Red Dragon's Keep. At need, they would answer the call to fight for the kingdom.

As time passed and peace ruled, or purely human wars raged, knowledge of your past was lost." She waved her hand at the Keep's inheritors.

She took a small sip of water from the wooden mug that she held. "Demons raided often, searching for what we didn't know." She shook her head, thinking of the talisman. *Best not to mention it here and now.*

"There were spells worked here that damped your power, so you never knew what you held within you. Those spells were broken when the Swords of Light were lifted. Each of you has gifts that we will train."

"You are some of the strongest mages in Ard Ri. With these gifts comes much danger. You will be targeted for ambush and assassination. That's what Jalyn and the others were trying to do to all of you. She, and they, failed because of the protections that the Dragons placed on Red Dragon's Keep." She paused, and then continued.

"I am a mage and a Dragon. I fought in the last war beside the Arachs. I will fight with you again in this one."

She threw her arms wide. "You are all my children."

Silent tension filled the forecourt.

Okay. So what do you say to a Dragon? The thought was reflected on everyone's face.

"Uh," Evan began. "Uh, so what do we call you and can you show us how you roast things?" he asked brightly. "Can you fly?"

The tension broke as everyone laughed a little hysterically.

"Yes, I can fly, and my name has always been Aeden. Lady Aeden to you, young scamp." Aeden laughed. "I'll show you soon, but not today. We all need rest."

Thomas raised his cup. "To Lady Aeden, a new old friend gladly welcome in this Keep. To all of us who vow to fight the Dark!"

Everyone raised their cups with a cheer and drank to the Dragon, and the Dragon's Children.

Chapter 33

Thomas sat with Marta at a table in the great hall. Ten awful days of burying the dead and burning Demon bodies, helping the wounded and cleaning up damage from the battle finally drew to a close.

Thomas picked up the mug of cider that he'd poured for himself and took a swallow. The sweet tartness of the drink made him feel better. It reminded him of seasons past.

Stone workers slowly entered the hall, finished for the day with repairs to the breaches in the Keep walls. They talked quietly among themselves as they poured drinks for themselves and took seats near the doors to the forecourt.

Thomas looked across the table at Marta. HellScream rested on the table next to HellReaver. "If my mother saw that," he nodded at the swords with a smile, "I wouldn't sit down for a month. She has a rule. 'No weapons on the table'."

Marta gave a tired smile. She'd been helping with the scrubbing and scraping in the Keep, removing the blood that had been spilled. "I think all mothers have that rule, including mine," she said.

Perhaps we could lean against the table. HellScream spoke sweetly in both of their minds. *Or we could lie on the bench.* HellReaver said drily.

"I hardly think it matters right now, since neither of them is here," Thomas said.

Raina walked into the great hall from the kitchen corridor carrying a cup of cider.

Thomas and Marta shared a startled look and hurriedly scooped up the swords and laid them on the benches next to them.

"I saw that," said Raina. She walked over to the table and sat next to Marta with a tired sigh. "I think we're finished with the cleaning."

HellReaver chuckled at Raina's observation. *No exceptions for Swords of Light?* He spoke in her mind as well. Raina gave a startled jerk and looked wide-eyed at Thomas and Marta. *Stop that,* HellScream scolded.

The three humans laughed. "I think so too, Raina," Thomas agreed with her. They sat in contented silence for a short time.

Raina finished her cider. "I'm going up to bed. Don't be long, Marta," she said, smiling knowingly at her daughter. She rose and stepped over the bench. "Would you take this back to the kitchen for me?"

"Of course, Mama. I'll be up shortly." She smiled at her mother. Raina slowly climbed the stairs, leaving the two of them alone.

"What happens now?" asked Marta quietly. "Do we stay here or do you want us to find somewhere else to stay?"

"I want all of you to stay here, of course," Thomas responded, his eyes widening. "I didn't know that you thought your family had to move. You've all helped us enormously. We came within a hair of losing this battle. Without you," he hesitated, "without *all* of us working together, I think we would have lost."

Marta shrugged and shook her head. "We just did what needed doing. Thank you for letting us stay. I've heard Mama and Da talking about what they thought you wanted them to do. Do you want me to tell them?"

"No," Thomas responded. "I'll tell Faolan the next time I see him. That will make it official. Not that you telling him isn't official, but..."

"I know what you mean," Marta said and chuckled.

"How are you doing?" Thomas asked. "I've been having some really bad dreams ever since the battle. Usually Demons eating my arms and legs. I wake up and fall asleep and wake up again and again during the night."

"Mine are of Demons coming out of the walls and killing everyone while we're sleeping," Marta mumbled. "I wish I knew how to make them stop," she exclaimed more loudly.

"I wonder how your da, or mine for that matter, got through this," Thomas wondered aloud. "Maybe he can help us. Let's talk to him in the morning."

"That's a good idea, Thomas," Marta said with approval. "What about the other children? I'll bet they're having the same problems."

"I heard Owen screaming night before last," Thomas replied. "Cameron and Evan are awfully quiet and Breanna is downright solemn. I hope your father has a solution."

"I can't believe Aeden is a Dragon," Marta changed the subject. She shook her head in astonishment. "That was the most incredible thing I've ever seen. When she changed the day after the battle to show us what she really is, I was truly shocked." Marta's eyes were wide in remembered wonder.

"I felt the same way," Thomas agreed. "She's always been here, as long as I can remember. I'm surprised that no one has noticed that she doesn't get old. Did she tell us how old she is? I can't remember." He turned the empty mug in his hands around and around and around.

Marta shook her head in denial. "No, I don't think she did. I don't think it matters, either. I'm just glad that at least one Dragon came to our aid."

"No question about that," Thomas agreed with her.

"Have you heard anything about your mother and father?" Marta laid a sympathetic hand on his.

He set the empty mug on the table. He reached out and took her hand in his. "No. That's been the hardest thing to bear. Not knowing. Maybe Lady Aeden can help. I'll ask if she can do some scouting from the air." He gave a crooked smile. "Can you imagine what will happen when she flies over the towns and villages? There'll be absolute panic!" He huffed a laugh. "Thanks for listening to me, Marta. I really needed to talk to someone."

"You're welcome, Thomas. We'll get through this. We just all need to stick together. She withdrew her hand from his and patted it. "I'm going up to bed. See you in the morning."

They both stood. "I'll put these in the kitchen," Thomas said, picking up the three empty mugs. "See you in the morning."

Marta turned and made her way up the stairs. Thomas took the mugs to the kitchen and sought his own bed.

Chapter 34

Mannan slammed his fists on the table in rage. *Nothing* was proceeding according to plan. He swept his arm across the table, sending parchment and spell books flying. He clasped his hands behind his back and stomped to the windows of his turret and back to the table. He fumed in anger to himself. His minions continually failed him.

The Arachs and Gobhlans had been ambushed and taken by Earl Tildon and his disgraced son, Garan. They were held in the dungeon of that minion's fiefdom. The dungeon had been spelled against all magic. And yet, the prisoners had escaped.

A Dragon had come to the aid of Red Dragon's Keep! The Swords of Light were awakened once again. His master would not be pleased.

He grabbed up a goblet of wine and drank deeply, then slammed the metal vessel back on the table, bending its stem.

Mannan turned. His blood red robes, bordered with spells in black, flared wide.

"Bring me the king's sorcerer," he ordered his slave, who knelt in the corner. Plans needed be advanced. The war *must* be won.

The slave hesitated.

"Go! Now!"

$ $ $

*The story continues in The Dragon's Children:
Book Two – Windward Range.*

Acknowledgements

Many people helped make this book possible. My sister Peg encouraged me every step of the way. My girls, Anne, Debbie and Jenni, helped me over the rough spots and said "Yes, you can."

Their husbands, Jeremy, Scott and Tom, listened while I talked and gave me some pretty good ideas.

My grandsons, Thomas, Owen, Cameron and Evan and my granddaughter Breanna – well, without them this story would not even have been created.

Many thanks to Andi Allott for keeping me grounded. Sherry Collins listened as I read her parts of the story over the phone. Susan Hicks read the story, and even though it's fantasy, really liked it.

To the members of AuthorU. They have been so supportive and given me so much feedback and inspiration. Red Dragon's Keep was a finalist in the '2016 Draft to Dream Contest' sponsored by AuthorU. The judges' critiques were invaluable.

To the Rocky Mountain Fiction Writers Aurora Critique Group, Susan, John, Amy, John, and Janet. Wow. They helped immeasurably with their critiques; they made Red Dragon's Keep a better story.

Characters

Duke Sir Thomas (Tom) Arach
Duchess Lady Jennifer Arach
Thomas Arach
Owen Arach
Breanna Arach
Lord John Arach
Lady Eirin Arach

Duke Sir Jeremy Gobhlan
Duchess Lady Anne Gobhlan
Cameron Gobhlan
Evan Gobhlan

Duke Sir Scott Windwalker
Duchess Lady Debra Windwalker

Lady Aeden - Dragon/Mage/Sword Mistress

Captain Braden - appointed captain of the guard after
Captain Mathin leaves
Captain Mathin - captain of the guard
Cathair Ri - The Kings City - Capital of Ard An Tir
Ciardha Demon - Demons of the Dark
Claiomh Solas - swords of light
       BattleSworn - Lord Tom Arach's sword
       FireGuard – Lady Jenni's sword
       GhostWalker - chooses Cameron
       HeartStriker- chooses Owen

HellReaver - chooses Thomas
HellScream - chooses Marta
OathKeeper - Aeden's sword
ShadowSworn - chooses Evan
SunWalker - chooses Breanna

Falcon's Spire - home of the Gobhlan's

Garan Tilden - squire, son of Earl Tildon of North Meall
Gregory – Red Dragon's Keep seneschal

Faolan Haloran - Steader, former Master Sergeant
Jaiman Haloran - son of Faolan
Kevin Haloran - son of Faolan
Marta Haloran – daughter of Faolan
Raina Haloran - Faolan's wife
Rand Haloran - grandfather of Marta

Jago – Gregory's clerk
Jalyn – head cook

Maccon - squire – friend
Mannan - High Draiolc - evil high wizard suborned by
          the Ciardha Demon
Moirra - the Keep wise woman/healer

North Meall - northern mounds – badlands – held by
          Earl Tilden and his son, Garan

Red Dragon's Keep - home of the Arachs

Seleigh Soren - Demon created by the High Draiolc to attack and kill those that are its designated prey.

Simon - chamberlain

Stefan - squire – friend

Tiarna Geal - Lords of Light

Windward Range - home of the WindWalkers

Dictionary

Aeden - Fire

Arach - Dragon

Ard An Tir - The Shining Lands Ard Ri - King's Land

An bhaile – (ahn wail) townsmen

Bolscaire bhaile – (bols care wail) town crier

Cailleach – (cal yish) - witch

Ciardha - (Kay r da) - the Dark - source of all Demons

Claiomh Solas - (Klay m So las) - Swords of Light

> BattleSworn
>
> FireGuard
>
> GhostWalker
>
> HeartStriker
>
> HellScream
>
> HellReaver
>
> OathKeeper
>
> ShadowCalled
>
> SunWalker

Cosain Morroin - (ko sane Mo ro in) - Shield Lands

Crionna baen - (kron a bay en) – Wise-woman

Cumhacht ar Draigoini – (come act ar drago in i)
Power of Dragons

Demon – (dayman) - Demon

Draiochta - (dray ok ta) - magic

Draiolc - (Dray olc) - dark wizard

Fuil - blood

Fuilba - (Fool ba) - dark bay color

Hold - small farm held by a holder

Holder - either indentured serf or small land holder be-
holden to a Steading
Ki - spiritual essence
Lands of Ard An Tir
Ard Ri - King's Land
Fearmhar (fear m har) - grasslands of the Horse
Lords
Talamh (Ta lem) - farmland Freeholders
Fasach (Fa sash) - desert Fanai – (fan eye)-
Nomads
Midach - (Mi dak) - doctor
Ri - (Ree) - King
Rivers
Banuisk
Caladen
Samphir
Sabhdan – (Say dan) – sultan, ruler
Salle - (Sal) - weapons training hall
Seleigh Soren - (Su lay so ren) - carnivorous Demon
compelled by magic to devour flesh and soul
Slieve Geal – (Sleeve Ga el) - Shining Mountain
Smachtmaistir – (Smawk t May stir) master Demon
controller
Steading - large land holding granted by the Lord to a
freeholder
Tiarna Geal - (Tee ar na Ga el) - Lords of Light

About the Author

Natli fell in love with science fiction when she 'borrowed' her father's copy of *Sixth Column* by Robert Heinlein. She was twelve. She was always the hero in the stories she wrote for herself. She thought she might be a veterinarian, a chemical engineer, or an astronaut.

She joined the Navy instead, and became a meteorologist and anti-submarine warfare specialist. She was the first woman assigned to the meteorology office at the Naval Air Station, Naha, Okinawa, Japan.

Natli designs websites, shows Shetland Sheepdogs and writes fantasy and science fiction. She has three girls, four grandsons and one granddaughter. Natli is a native Coloradan and lives in Aurora, Colorado.

She would love to have a Dragon for a friend. She enjoys quilting, target practice, riding, and jumping out of perfectly good airplanes. Next is learning how to sword fight.

(She still has that paperback copy of *Sixth Column*)

Other Titles by Natli VanDerWerken

The Dragon's Children: Windward Range
(Book 2 forthcoming)

The Dragon's Children: DreamWalker
(Book 3 forthcoming)

The Dragon's Children: Falcon's Spire
(Book 4 forthcoming)

The Dragon's Children: Talisman
(Book 5 forthcoming)

Connect with Natli VanDerWerken

Thanks for reading my books. I enjoy hearing from all of you.

Meet me on my website at
http://www.natlivanderwerken.com
You can also find me on Facebook at
facebook.com/Natli VanDerWerken-Author
Email me at natli@natlivanderwerken.com
If you liked Red Dragon's Keep, please leave a review at Amazon.com. Every review is important, both for placement and for your thoughts about the book. I read every one of them.